Basecraft Cirrostratus

by Rose LaCroix

Basecraft Cirrostratus

Copyright © Rose LaCroix
2010, 2014

Cover Artwork by Myenia

Published by FurPlanet
Dallas, Texas
www.furplanet.com

ISBN 978-1-61450-219-7

Printed in the United States of America
Second Edition Trade Paperback 2014

Table of Contents

To my love and inspiration, known to fans, friends, and in my heart as the
One and only Kobi LaCroix.

Acknowledgments

Many thanks go to Whyteyote, who offered very helpful advice in improving this book;

To Dan (Quinn Yellowfox) for his correspondence and encouragement;

To my father, for helping spark my interests in history and aviation;

To Reagan (Sulaco) for a tremendous amount of visual inspiration by way of his art;

To Myenia, for creating such a gorgeous cover graphic;

And to Matt (Kobi) simply for being there.

Prologue

We should have known that Salaar was a megalomaniac who would stop at nothing to get his way. We should have been alarmed when we were urged, in light of imaginary dangers, to surrender our freedom and submit to his will. We should have stood against him and firmly, with one voice, rejected his vision of total control. Ah, but isn't hindsight grand? Looking back the path we were on seemed so clear, but it certainly seemed less so in those days.

I am reminded of a cruel experiment I read of once as a student. Two frogs were placed in pots of water. One pot was heated immediately to scalding temperature, and the frog struggled and leapt free of the water before it could be boiled to death. The other pot was heated gradually, such that the frog in that pot never knew or sensed it was in danger until it finally met its doom. That was how it happened; each time the reins of power were tightened, we were allowed to get comfortable until one day when we awoke to find ourselves powerless.

King Brannagh IX, young and inexperienced heir to the throne of Greater Lutro-Vulpes, had just come to power when an explosion at the Dai-Yel petrochemical plant in Lutrum killed fourteen workers and leveled a large part of the city. Our minister of the interior at the time, a wolf named Salaar Avys, blamed the explosion on a group of wayward youths who had been seduced to crime by a lenient society; though almost everyone at the plant that day knew it was a bad valve on a steam pipe, no one argued.

A group of four local boys -known more for their bad reputation than for any actual misdeeds- was summarily rounded up and, in a very public way, shot in front of the devastated plant as an audience of onlookers watched one cold morning. The king, who had never believed their guilt, had been convinced by

1

Minister Avys' requests to sign an order waiving their right to a trial by jury. He had to make an example, the minister told him, and a ruler so young and inexperienced as himself could not risk looking weak before the world.

From that day on, Minister Avys became a force to be reckoned with in our government. His influence over the king grew until it was clear that Minister Avys wielded the real power.

He urged the king to begin a vast modernization initiative, and commissioned the building of a system of high-speed highways called Hyperways between all of the kingdom's major cities. He also commissioned the building of a new administrative and industrial capital, New Lycopolis, which was the first modern purpose-built city in the land. The newsreels proudly showed King Brannagh reviewing parades from a stand high above the broad streets of the new city... with Minister Avys standing closely by.

Perhaps the most amazing part of this initiative, though, was its focus on aviation. Pilots' licenses became easier to obtain, and the government commissioned a series of gigantic flying airstrips known as basecraft. But for Salaar Avys, none of this would ever be enough.

From the Dai-Yel explosion onward, he campaigned aggressively for reform, claiming the government's hands were tied by the constitution and its promises of due process while criminals and miscreants ran free, threatening the very fabric of society. He pushed for the formation of a central police force that answered only to the highest levels of government. He criticized the monarchy for allowing poverty to run rampant in the cities. Most of all, he raged on with a passion about how the secular state had lost its moral compass and fallen away from the true vision of the Book of Inakara, and the sainted martyr and prophet Ovego.

His speeches, of course, had no merit, but those of us who knew better were either silent, or were met by ears that would not hear and eyes that would not see. His charisma was unstoppable, and in a landslide election, Interior Minister Avys became prime minister in the year 1694 of the Era of Kingdoms.

Later that same year, the young king, all of 16 years old, abdicated. It was done with the exact sort of vapid pageantry Minister Avys adored, with guards and courtiers in traditional costume, a band of royal guards to sound the fanfare, and an invitation to the world press to witness the event. The cameras, of course, dutifully recorded the entire abdication ceremony, the stroke of the pen, the cordial handshake, and the lavish banquet afterward.

What they did not show was the young king hastily running for his limousine and fleeing for his life shortly after the ceremony, or his being grazed by an assassin's bullet as he ran across the apron at Grand Lutrum Airfield, boarding a flight for the Isle of Rest.

The exiled young king never arrived at the Isle of Rest. Some say he lives on in the belly of a basecraft, where many outlaws now hide from Emperor Salaar's secret police, the Nightwatch. Others say he was stabbed to death on his flight to the Isle of Rest and thrown into the ocean... a much more likely scenario.

Salaar Avys, now called Emperor Salaar, wasted no time in having his way with the country. As one who preached a peculiar mix of strict state control and free and open economic policy, he soon found ways to make all of his views manifest and to shape the new regime in his own image.

The press and media, as well as all film, books, newspapers, and television were taken quickly under his control. Panels were set up to approve all content that might be watched, read, or heard by subjects of the new regime, and contracts were given to preferred companies to produce and market all state-approved media.

All market regulation, meanwhile, was done away with. Imports and exports now flow freely, a tactic that Salaar uses to keep our would-be rescuers in nations like Lycocia pacified.

Small companies have been forced out of business one by one, each one of them bought out and sometimes liquidated by four companies... each of which is run by friends, relatives, and acquaintances of Emperor Salaar. Those who wished to keep any profits from their business did best to become a franchise of a larger company, or else risk losing everything.

One of the larger companies' favorite tactics was to file an anti-trust suit against a smaller competitor; because the courts now rule not by jury but by one judge's decision, it was no trouble to bring all the judges to the side of these larger companies.

With the courts now no obstacle to convictions and due process a thing of the past, the list of punishable crimes grew longer. It immediately became a crime to deny the Inakara faith or to teach anything contrary to its teachings in schools and universities.

In 1695, it became a crime for couples of different species or the same sex to be seen in public, then in 1701 the law even pursued us into the privacy of our own homes. One can no longer even trust their own neighbors; crimes can be reported anonymously now, and often are.

All drinks stronger than wine were outlawed. Growing, selling, or smoking ghella leaves, already illegal, became capital offenses. All weapons were banned from public ownership; even kitchen knives more than finger-length now must bear a stamped serial number and be registered with local police; an unregistered kitchen knife is easily a death sentence.

Salaar promised that we would never see poverty again, but his promise came at a terrible price. His regime did nothing at all to help the poor; those who were unable to work due to some illness of the body or mind simply vanished, and we can only assume those poor souls are no longer with us.

Those who were more able were shuttled off to the cities where hastily-built block flats awaited them. They were pressed into service with various factory jobs, at all times walled off from the view of the upper and middle classes. Each day now they trudge through underground corridors to and from their windowless homes, forbidden to set foot in any place where the rest of us might see them.

The emperor was also quick to make his mark on the map, changing the entire face of the former Greater Lutro-Vulpes. In 1699 the official capital was moved from Lutrum to Highridge. Shortly thereafter, the expansion grew rapidly. The Great

Wolven Imperium began, and Tavell was annexed along with Orientania and all of the major outlying islands. We are now nearly the size of the Kanil empire from long ago, and not a single shot has been fired... At least, not publicly. Those of us who have not yet completely shut off our minds cannot help but notice the large number of bombers flying toward the highlands of Tartús, where some resistance to the Imperium survives.

Salaar is shameless in promoting the few positive changes he has brought about. True, most of us now have vehicles; those of us unable to afford an expensive touring car can at least buy, through a program of stamps and earned credits, a Lutra Special. It is also true that he modernized the currency from the archaic three-tier system of the Sol, Luna, and Terra to a decimal two-tier system of one hundred Imperials to one Crown. This is to say nothing of the initiatives begun while he was still an elected minister.

But to those who speak so glowingly of how good their life is now, I ask, was it really worth these few comforts to sacrifice all our liberty and dignity? Was it worth risking being taken from your home one night for a crime you didn't commit, then shot without ever knowing why? Was it worth the life of an unlucky young king who only wanted the best for his country?

Life goes on, but for those of us whose will is not completely broken, we wait for our moment to strike. Our would-be rescuers in other lands are either subdued by threats of force or sated by an abundance of cheap exports.

Ultimately, only those of us who have lived the nightmare can awaken our nation from it. If an organized resistance exists somewhere on a remote island or in the belly of a basecraft, I shall join, and if I am captured in seeking or fighting for them, let this written record show that I did exist, I had a life, I had thoughts and feelings and a purpose... and that if I am killed before the Great Wolven Imperium is no more, I shall curse the tyrant Salaar with my dying breath.

From the journal of Elor Kaya, 1704 E.K.

CHAPTER ONE
Farewell To Highridge

Elor scanned his eyes across the small bedroom of his flat and frowned. He had made his decision, he was leaving that very day, and the airliner that would, supposedly, take him to Archer's Cove was one of the few flights that made that one connecting stop he needed.

All the signs had told him that his time was growing very short. The way the other professors had begun to shun him, the way local police had begun stopping him and asking his business, and the way all of his mail had been very messily opened and re-sealed... these were all ominous signs that he was under suspicion. After a Nightwatch agent had confronted him outside the lecture hall shortly after one of his classes and demanded to see the lesson plan, he promptly booked his flight and secured travel papers.

Now he had just four scant hours to gather as much as he could fit into two suitcases and drive to the airport twenty kilometers outside the city... and hopefully catch his flight before the Nightwatch realized he was getting away.

It was the 8th of Lai, the 5th month of the year in the Kanil calendar, and through the open window the gentle, cool breeze that blew across the city of Highridge wafted gracefully in. Papers laying strewn on Elor's bed and desk fluttered gently as the panther paced restlessly about his room, scanning for any items too important to leave behind.

An alarm clock... Did he really need that? It wasn't as if he couldn't find another one. The tan-furred panther picked it up, frowning a bit, before placing it back on the nightstand.

Next to the alarm clock stood a portrait of himself with a

wolf, some years younger than he, standing together at a festival near the old medieval gates of Lutrum. He picked it up, trying to remove it from the heavy frame, but the back of the frame was bent from a previous tumble off the nightstand. He looked at his watch again. Fuck, just over three hours! He smashed the glass of the frame against the corner of the nightstand and pulled the picture out, rolling it up and tucking it into the inner pocket of his jacket.

What else? He didn't have many books left; most of his books had been seized a few months ago when the Ministry of Communications audited the offices of university officials. All Elor had was an old political science book... one that was not party-approved and not the sort of thing he wanted to be caught with on an airliner. He opened the window of his bedroom and threw it out. It fell neatly down, three floors in the narrow alleyway below, landing closed with its front cover facing up.

Elor ran through the checklist of what he had so far. Clothing. Basic toiletries. Sixty Crowns in banknotes and seventy-two Imperials in coins. His state ID papers. His state-approved travel voucher for domestic air travel. His tickets. He nodded, trying not to think of any of the trinkets and niceties that he would normally have taken if moving for good; they would only hinder him.

His suitcases bulging, he looked at the time. Only two hours left! How did the time get away from him?

Never mind, he thought to himself as he hurriedly grabbed the two suitcases and headed for his front door. He pulled it shut behind him, even bothering to lock the door as if he were only going for a short time. Down the hallway to the stairs he walked, out to the street where his car waited. He normally kept it parked in a garage a few blocks away, but for today had parked it just on the curb in front of the building. He popped a few small brass snaps and rolled back the tiny green Lutra Special's roof, then hastily threw the heavy suitcases in the tiny back seat before climbing in and starting the engine.

A few minutes later, as he left the surface streets of Greater Highridge for the H-51 beltway around the city, he was relieved to see the traffic moving at a steady pace. Perhaps he had prepared for a long drive for nothing, but never mind; better early than late. Besides, there were good reasons for not waiting until the last minute in this day and age.

Back in Highridge, four creatures, a wolf, a marten, a fox, and a ferret, all dressed in black suits with black overcoats and bowler hats, stood at the door of an apartment, each carrying a small semi-automatic pistol. They were after a creature named one of the most dangerous intellectuals in the Imperium, one who had somehow managed to teach subversive and illegal theories on the sly for more than eight years and somehow never get caught.

Already they had let far too many dangerous intellectuals slip through their fingers, and the agents of the Nightwatch, an elite secret police force who answered only to the emperor, were not about to let this one get away.

"Open the door! You don't have to make this any harder! Surrender and you might survive!" the ferret shouted. There was no answer. He gave a nod to the fox, who took a small hatchet from under his coat and began brutally hacking away at the wood around the doorknob. One kick from the taller, stronger wolf and the door gave with a loud crack.

The agents fanned out, guns drawn, the fox wielding his hatchet in his left hand while in his right hand, his finger rested nervously on the trigger of his pistol. The four searched the apartment thoroughly, finding no sign of Elor. They checked closets, under beds, and even the walls and floors for secret doors... absolutely nothing.

"Fuck! He's gone!" the marten shouted, jamming his gun back into a shoulder holster.

"We need to find him fast, this one's a flight risk," the ferret said. He nodded to the fox. "You, find a call box and phone the chief. Tell him we've got a fugitive on our hands and we need to know where he's gone."

The fox saluted smartly and ran down the stairs. "You, get the car warmed up," he said to the wolf, who obeyed.

"And you, stay here with me, maybe there's some clue to

where he's gone in this building. Search everything," he said to the marten, who immediately began to tear the room apart.

* * *

Elor exited the Hyperway and drove down a narrow, two-lane road that ran through farmers' fields for about three kilometers before reaching the gates of a fenced-off lot marked "long-term parking." He calmly parked his car, taking out the suitcases, then carefully rolled the rubberized canvas roof back in place to protect the car's interior. Whoever bought it second-hand from a seized property auction would at least have a dry seat to sit on.

He began walking toward the terminal, a small building of white stucco, glass brick, and chrome about one hundred meters away, monitoring every step to make sure he didn't betray that he was running for his life. He gave his fedora a rakish cock, plucking up his courage as he entered the terminal through a revolving door and approached the ticket counter, his ticket in hand.

"On holiday?" the clerk, a pretty white-tail doe asked. Elor smiled and nodded.

"Yes, Archer's Cove," he said calmly.

"Have all your papers, Mr. Kaya?" she asked.

He calmly presented his papers, and the clerk made a small note in a log book. "Your plane is that white and red one there, Archer's Cove Excursions flight 11. Boarding begins in about one hour. Do make yourself comfortable!"

Elor nodded politely and made his way to the lobby area. There was nothing to do for now, and the panther decided it was best to find some food. At one side of the lobby was a lunch counter, but it was far too expensive for his liking; then again, he realized it might be some time before he ate again if they didn't serve any food on the flight. He sat down and ordered a bowl of potato and onion soup and a glass of ice water; hardly the finest meal he could hope for, but he had to mind his budget.

As he ate, Elor thumbed through a newspaper another diner had left on the counter. As usual, it offered nothing but the same mix of glowing propaganda and hateful vitriol. A moral panic story about ghella leaf usage being "widespread" among young boys graced the front page, just below a story praising Salaar for an increase in domestic productivity for the tenth year in a row.

Elor sighed. The farce he was leaving behind seemed to make his destination seem more appealing. He turned on the swiveling stool, gazing out through the tall windows across the apron where airliners of every shape and description sat parked.

"Enjoy your soup?" the young fennec behind the counter asked, his large ears twitching comically as he grinned.

"Yes, thank you," Elor replied. "That was how much?"

"Two Crowns fifteen," said the fennec. Elor's tail twitched slightly at this; a comparable meal at any small cafe in Highridge would cost about 50 Imperials. He reached into his pocket and pulled out a Five crown note, handing it to the fennec, who promptly gave him his change.

"Thank you, have a nice day!" the fennec said as Elor left the counter and strode over to the lobby.

* * *

The dispatcher at the Nightwatch Headquarters, Sector HR9 Greater Highridge, looked nervous. In his hands were two telephone receivers, one of them connected to a very nervous agent in a police call box in downtown Highridge, and one with the Ministry of Transport and Travel Safety, the agency who issued travel clearances. Trouble was, the MTTS agent on the other line was, himself, on two lines at the same time, talking to no fewer than two field offices at a time to try to find out if any of them had issued state clearance for one Elor Kaya to travel recently.

After half an hour of bickering about procedure and long delays, none other than the MTTS agency for sector HR9 (who the Nightwatch had to contact through MTTS headquarters in New Lycopolis because inter-agency dealing between field offices was forbidden) confirmed what the agent feared. He ran around the corner to tell the wolf to get the car started, then ran

11

up the stairs in the apartment building.

"We've got 45 minutes before he leaves, he's at the airport, let's go!" the fox shouted. The ferret and marten wasted no time. All three bolted downstairs and piled into the older touring car, and in moments they were roaring down the entrance ramp to the H-51, tires squealing as they barely made the turn.

The passengers for flight 11 had begun to line up. Pre-flight checks had gone smoothly, and boarding had begun a few minutes early. Elor handed the attendant his ticket at the door and strode out onto the apron without difficulty, walking to the moderately-sized, sleek propeller-driven plane. It was an LV-10 Vanguard, a very fast airliner that would have no trouble getting to Archer's Cove in just a few hours, even with a stop 50 kilometers offshore on the deck of the basecraft Cirrostratus. As the panther boarded the plane, he looked back for just a moment with sadness in his eyes. Perhaps, he thought, this was his last time feeling the confident firmness of solid ground beneath his feet. This was truly a moment for reflection...

...No, later. He couldn't hold up the line and he certainly couldn't afford to act suspiciously. The panther took his seat and lay back, staring at the headliner and waiting for the sound of the engines to tell him he was safe at last.

The heavy touring car slewed wildly through traffic, a crude, motor-driven siren sounding as the wolf navigated a terrifying course down the H51 toward the H-5 and the airport beyond. He suddenly stood on the brakes, causing the nose of the car to dip heavily and the other three agents to fly forward, the marten chipping a tooth on the car's metal dash panel. Ahead were two heavy mining trucks that had just pulled onto the Hyperway and blocked both lanes, traveling far slower than the rest of the traffic. One of the drivers, hearing the siren behind, tried to maneuver into the other lane, but clipped the corner of the other truck, sending it into a guard rail. The two massive trucks seemed to collide over and over like a pair of angry titans before one careened down a soft shoulder and overturned, spilling a huge amount of ore. The other truck was now sideways across both lanes of the carriageway, with the terrified agents just behind, having barely missed being part of this horrendous crash.

As other motorists rushed to help the two truck drivers, the wolf gunned the engine and began trying to find a way around the twisted wreck, each time being blocked either by wreckage, spectators, or another car. Fully ten minutes passed before he could finally advance far enough to travel down the median, nearly getting the car stuck in the soft ground before pulling back onto the road, sirens blaring.

As the plane began to move forward, Elor heard sirens and saw an older touring car caked in mud pulling onto the apron, with four Nightwatch agents piling out. The plane sped up and was soon off the ground as the four agents stood, looking in silent desperation at their quarry's escape. One agent, a wolf, threw his hat on the ground, stomping it furiously.

Yet another high-profile criminal had evaded the long arm of the law... the Nightwatch command was not going to be happy.

CHAPTER TWO
The Cunning Little Vixen

The sun began to set as the sleek airliner passed over the sea coast of the Great Wolven Imperium. Far below, the lights of the twin cities of Foxport and Northarhour, two cities on opposite sides of the same natural harbor that straddled two provinces, began to turn on as sunlight faded from view on the ground below. High overhead, where Elor gazed thoughtfully out the window, the sunset lingered far longer.

Many of the passengers in the cabin seemed content to catch a few moments of sleep, but for Elor there was no such luxury. His mind began to drift, as it often did when lying awake in bed, to thoughts of his beloved Vinz.

From the moment they met at a small newsstand just a short walk from the University of Lutrum, Vinz and Elor had been inseparable. Elor, then 27, was a graduate student in science education. Vinz, only 19 at the time, was a second-year diction and language therapy student. They would meet at the newsstand regularly between classes, chatting, sometimes going to a nearby café if time allowed.

Over the following weeks they became more friendly, studying together, going to the cinema, and going out for meals, but neither thought of the other as more than just a friend until one fateful night in the middle of that spring semester.

They had been out at dinner, and it was unseasonably cold that night. Elor kept rubbing his hands together. "Cold, isn't it?" Vinz said.

"It will be. The heat's not working in my dormitory," Elor said, tail twitching.

Vinz hesitated a moment. "My flat's heater works," he said before he could really think about what it meant.

The panther's expression perked. "Does it?" he said, after a moment's hesitation.

"Yes..." said Vinz, ears back, fidgeting somewhat.

"That's nice," said Elor, his tone wary.

Oh please, let him ask! Thought Elor, terrified to impose, his heart racing in his chest.

"You could... That is... If you don't mind... I have no plans and..." Vinz said, starting to blush under his fur.

"And?" said Elor, reaching out to touch Vinz's hand and gazing at the wolf intently, his eyes pleading.

Come on you fool! Elor thought silently to himself as he watched the light from the gas streetlights create halos in Vinz's fur, their combined breath creating a dreamlike haze in the air.

Vinz smiled. "It's this way," he said, grabbing Elor's hand and practically dragging him the three blocks home.

The first night passed without much happening between them. They fell asleep in each other's arms, with little more than a loving caress passing between them in the hours before dawn. When sunrise came each bade the other farewell... and each vowed, however silently, that the other would be his own.

As the months drew on, they began to see each other more, but approached their feelings with caution. Elor was no innocent when it came to males, but with Vinz it always seemed different, special, and something that he never wanted to force or rush. It was fully a week after their first night together before Elor and Vinz had the courage to see each other unclothed, and three more days before they began to explore, ever so carefully at first, the pleasures of each other's warm, well-built bodies.

Elor could still recall what a terrifying, exciting feeling it was the first time he had let Vinz mount him, and the intense electric thrill that ran through his body as the wolf, still locked inside him, bent double and began to pleasure him with his tongue.

Their relationship remained a secret, but not a well-kept one. To almost everyone that knew them, it was obvious from the outset that Vinz and Elor were mad for each other, and no

16

one needed to see them naked and entwined to figure it out.

Most of the faculty and students made snide remarks behind their backs, but that was hardly the worst of their worries. When Imperial Order 313 was passed in 1695, requiring all "male-alike couples and individuals demonstrating strange and unhealthy attractions to their like sex" to keep all signs of their life from public view, Vinz saw the writing on the wall. He knew that it was only a matter of time before the new regime came for them, regardless of how much they tried not to draw attention to themselves.

Never mind that they never actually admitted or displayed their relationship; in the eyes of the Great Wolven Imperium, they were already living too publicly simply because their peers *knew about them.*

Vinz wanted to flee to some place more friendly, and begged Elor to join him, but Elor refused; he was in the middle of preparing his thesis, well on his way, at the age of only 29, to becoming a professor of biology, and he wasn't going to lose that.

"You don't understand," Vinz would say, his eyes wide with concern. "It's been like this for all of history, first they come after you when you show yourself in public, then they decide they don't want to wait. They'll pass another law and they'll come for us in our own homes. Then they'll pass another law saying they don't even have to try us. We'll be shot in the streets, Elor."

"You're being unreasonable," Elor replied. "We'll be fine, this is all just some busybodies in the government trying to make the people think they're doing something. They probably won't even prosecute anyone under this law, and they're certainly not going to kill anyone for this."

"Maybe I am being unreasonable, but I don't want to wait and find out," Vinz said. "I'm leaving this place the first chance I get. Are you coming?"

"I don't know, Vinz," said Elor, sighing, his shoulders sagging. "I need some time. I've got my thesis in only a few days. Let me do this, at least, please?"

Vinz didn't wait for his lover. He left the night before Elor handed in his thesis. All he left was a brief note:

Unable to get travel papers to leave the country.
Gone to Basecraft Cirrostratus.
See you when you get your wits about you.

Love,
Vinz

Elor had shredded that note with his bare claws and thrown the pieces out the window that night... now he fervently wished he still had that note, that final scrap of what he'd lost. He'd be lucky if Vinz even remembered him at all; asking for the relationship to continue as it had been was asking far too much.

Now he too was on the run, only for him, the escape was a close shave and not a clean getaway. He'd avoided charges of perversion and crimes against Imperial integrity for his relationship with Vinz, but now he faced charges of indoctrination against the Imperium for too many mentions of evolutionary theory in his lectures, not to mention libel against the Imperium, antisocial activity, and sedition in speaking. If brought to trial, the courts would probably add formal charges of unnatural and unholy acts (and whatever else they could accuse him of) to seal his death sentence. It wasn't a matter of whether or not he'd be found guilty, but how they'd dispose of him.

One thing was for sure: he had nothing to lose by trying to find Vinz again. His life as he knew it was effectively over, and anything or anyone from the life he had known might provide some much-needed comfort.

Soon, a voice crackled over a cheap speaker. "This is your pilot speaking, we are currently holding, due for arrival on the Basecraft Cirrostratus in about one half hour. For those of you continuing on to Archer's Cove, remember that our flight leaves on schedule, not based on our passenger list, so you will be left if you are not on the plane at 22:16. For those of you changing flights or whose final destination is the Cirrostratus, we thank you for flying Archer's Cove Excursions. Current conditions on the deck of the basecraft are light fog with a visibility of 900 meters, winds less than 2 knots with gusts up to 14, and temperature about 2 degrees aquagrade."

Such conditions were actually very good for a night-time landing on a basecraft. Even at the relatively low altitude of 3km, near-freezing temperatures and harsh winds were the rule and not the exception. Of course, for safety reasons, landings were never attempted on basecraft and all aircraft on board were lowered into hangars below decks when the wind speed exceeded a sustained 18 knots, or when the temperature went more than 20 degrees below freezing.

The small plane lurched as the pilot nosed down slightly, losing altitude. The mist outside the windows became thicker, until it was difficult to see past the wing of the plane. Suddenly a roar could be heard as the landing gear began to swing into place from within their cowled nacelles, and the lights of the massive Basecraft Cirrostratus could at last be seen.

The Basecraft Cirrostratus, at slightly over a kilometer long, 200 meters high, and 300 meters wide, was the largest craft of her type, typically circling between the Isle of Rest and Archer's Cove, and always within the zones that, according to Imperial law, were exempt from many of the rigorous moral codes on the surface. Her airframe, put into service on the day Salaar Avys became emperor, was designed to go eighteen years without maintenance, and still had a good eight years left before coming back to the surface for inspection. If an engine broke down, all engines were stopped and a crew was brought up to her; if she needed fuel, a smaller airship, a tanker, brought all she needed. All supplies, all crew, all parts and services came through the sky. The Basecraft Cirrostratus was, for all intents and purposes, a city apart from the earth.

Within her bowels were not only tanks for housing the vital K-39 fuel that powered every aircraft in the Imperium and beyond, but also restaurants, a hotel, shops, and even long-term residences. Of course, most visitors rarely went below the first sublevel, the hangar level where a few snack stands, shops, restrooms, and a small hotel were situated. Below these, further into the inner workings of the massive ship, was where things got really interesting.

It was this shadow world that Elor was thinking of as the plane landed on the wide expanse of the deck. The airliner touched down with a screech of rubber, a slight sideways lurch, and finally a forward dive as the drag line caught a specially-made hook in the tail of the craft. The hook then disengaged and the plane began to taxi into an apron area just beside the bridge of the basecraft.

As the plane came to a stop, passengers restlessly began grabbing their belongings, standing and moving toward the door at the right rear of the plane. A clunk followed by a soft sucking sound could be heard as the door was opened and lowered, forming a set of stairs. Passengers piled out onto the cold, windswept apron atop the basecraft, then promptly made their way toward a small door in the side of the large tower located on the ship's port side, midway down its length. One passenger's hat flew away, and the young genet ran after it in vain, stopping short as she saw it take to the black night sky, lost forever.

Elor tried not to look too eager to get off the plane, but his quickened pace was noticeable as he made his way to the door and down the stairs to the hangar deck, suitcases in hand. He paused a moment as he reached the deck, then looked at his surroundings. On either side of the staircase stood a long arcade of shops, snack stands, restaurants, and other utilities, all well-lit and well-traveled. Before him, in a dark expanse, stood the hangar, a vast open space with only a few dim gas arc lights. He could make out the vague forms of the various aircraft there, from small biplanes to fast, light, and probably illegal craft that appeared to be modified fighter-interceptors with bright, garish paint schemes. There was even a Tannawani Autogyro, a rare craft built in Lycocia that hadn't been produced in about fifteen years.

A sign could be seen between two rows of lots in the hangar area, somewhat faint and battered. It read "To Sub-Levels 2-5: Sub-Levels 6-9 off limits to public." This was the sign he was looking for. He walked cautiously down the aisle between the hangar lots, some empty and some filled with just about any aircraft imaginable. The vast expanse seemed to go on forever, the path before him always just out of visual range, until finally he arrived at a wall. There, a sign with a pictogram of stairs and an arrow pointed the way. Just a short walk from there, a single red bulb hummed away in its shielded cage-style industrial fixture next to a narrow hatchway. Elor could barely fit through the narrow opening, let lone get his suitcases through.

Inside was an equally tight stairway of steep, narrow ladders, stretching down as far as the eye could see. Elor was headed for sublevel 5, as far into the belly of the ship as he could go without a crew pass, and most importantly of all, the home of the Cunning Little Vixen.

The Cunning Little Vixen was a jazz and whiskey bar, nothing more or less. Any surface-dweller's attempt to color it in more florid terms was motivated either by ignorant romanticism or embarrassment at having been there. It was a sleazy, seedy, disreputable place where fights were frequent, life was cheap, and sex was easy... no matter what kind you were looking for.

The only extraordinary thing about it was the fact that it had opened after such establishments had long been banned on the surface; this was literally one of the last of its kind. Other jazz and whiskey bars had since sprung up on other basecraft, of course; the Basecraft Cumulus had the Frisky Wolf, and the Basecraft Nimbostratus had the Gold Tooth, and the Basecraft Altocirrus had the Fiddle and Hedgehog, but none of these were nearly as famous- or infamous- as the Cunning Little Vixen.

It was here that the infamous Culture Crime Collective was formed, a group of intellectuals, artists, filmmakers, authors, and thinkers who had all come together to share resources and support. If anyone would know where a former aspiring speech therapist with a penchant for older males and a permissive stance on politics was, they certainly would.

Down the stairs Elor trudged, struggling to keep his belongings with him as he clambered down the narrow rungs of the near-vertical descent into the growing darkness of the ship.

Gravity pulled him downward, vertigo pulled him outward, but his sheer force of will held him steady for those last few flights of stairs.

It was not a sign for sublevel 5 but the sound of jazz music that told the panther he had arrived at the correct level. He stepped through a narrow doorway, much like the one on sublevel 1, once again having a difficult time pulling his suitcases through.

Unlike the relative calm of the hangar, the sight that greeted him was quite a shock. Below a sky of steam pipes and gas arc lights stood the streets of a shanty town, a thriving ghetto deep in the heart of this massive aircraft. Street vendors sold hot sausages, children in threadbare clothes ran around his feet, and a bicycle whizzed by before the rider could even ring his bell. All around were shops and houses built out of found materials, mostly the wood from engine shipping crates. Above, clotheslines and light bulbs on lines crisscrossed the street. It was almost as alive as the poor neighborhoods he remembered from years ago, the ones that Emperor Salaar had walled off to keep the poor factory workers out of sight and out of mind.

Toward the end of this narrow alleyway stood a building quite unlike the others. If it was a haphazard collection of old shipping crates underneath, its facade certainly hid it well. Stucco, chrome, and a pink neon sign festooned with a buxom caricature of a winking fox marked this as the Cunning Little Vixen, the very center of life in this strange new underworld- an underworld, Elor reminded himself, that he had little choice but to call home.

The panther wasn't sure what he would find. The Vixen, as it was called, was a hangout for nearly everyone, which made for some very uneasy encounters. Everyone had their little corner of the club, from the artists and jazz musicians to the Cylinderheads, a dangerous gang who often terrorized outlaw and citizen alike. The fact was, they were only welcome in The Vixen for two reasons: they supplied the precious bootleg alcohol that kept them in business, and the simple fact that they decided they liked it there.

When the Cylinderheads decided they liked a place, they

didn't leave.

Elor plucked up his courage and walked through the surprisingly well-balanced revolving door at the front of the club. To his right was a long bar, accented with the same blend of chrome and neon as the facade. This seemed to be where all the unsavory characters clustered. There was a canine of some sort who wore on the sleeve of his brown leather jacket the distinctive badge of a Cylinderhead: a wolf skull pierced by a two-bladed propeller and the initials "V.B.B." beneath it. The initials stood for "Victory by Blood," a motto the Cylinderheads took very seriously.

The canine turned his head and glared at Elor, who wisely turned his eyes away from this silent challenge. He walked quickly toward a doorway on his left, where he could hear a rollicking piano tune being played amid the sounds of clubgoers.

There, in the dimly-lit room filled with the smoke from pipes, cigars, and cigarettes (some of which exuded more than a hint of ghella leaf), was a fairly large music hall with tables, chairs, and a stage some distance away. On the edge of the room there were booths, and it seemed each booth was its own microcosm of the sorts of creatures that made their homes in the basecraft.

One booth was full of young males, each impeccably groomed, wearing sleeveless shirts and caps, some with different colored feathers. The panther knew all too well what this meant; in his younger days, before he had met Vinz, Elor had worn a bright blue feather in his cap meaning he was a "versatile" male when frequenting some of the seedier clubs that once filled the back alleys of Highridge before the days of the Imperium. A pink feather was the sign of a submissive, and a red feather was a dominant male. A myriad of other colored articles and jewelry told all sorts of fascinating information of interest to those who were looking for a male partner for the night. Their favorite positions, age, experience, and even specific fetishes were communicated in a complex language of colors and symbols.

Elor, of course, had quit that scene after meeting Vinz, but the sight of these boys made him at once sad that he had left it behind and hopeful that such a scene still existed long after it had been blotted from the surface world. Perhaps, too, Elor felt more than a little sorry he didn't have time to get more acquainted with a very good-looking young tiger who winked at him admiringly.

Finally he arrived at a booth where a group sat around, keeping a conversation that was both animated and a bit tense, filled with both energy and anger, passion and frustration. Elor looked them over, then his heart leapt as he saw a face he recognized.

The badger looked somewhat older, the last decade having not been kind to him, but sure enough, there sat Gilyar Honyo, the revolutionary filmmaker and one of the reasons Vinz had fled to this basecraft to begin with. Gilyar had been one of the first to set up refuge on the basecraft and founded the Culture Crime Collective, after calling Salaar's regime "poison injected into the heart of reason" and covertly distributing a very incendiary film satirizing Emperor Salaar.

He and Vinz had somehow struck up a correspondence in the months after Order 313 was passed, Gilyar's letters being handed off to various clubgoers who then mailed them from the surface for a small tip, and Elor could only guess that of all the creatures in the club, he was the most likely to know Vinz particularly well at this point.

Elor straightened his tie and adjusted his collar as he approached the booth. At first, no one there acknowledged him. He then cleared his throat. A few of them looked his way. "Pardon me," he began, unsure how to word his question. "Erm... There's a... I'm looking for... Have any of you seen this wolf?" Elor reached into his pocket and unrolled the picture, showing it to everyone at the booth.

"Well, now, that depends," Gilyar said, "Who wants to know?"

The panther sat down on the edge of the softly-padded bench seat of the booth. "I am Professor Elor Kaya, late of University College Highridge, though I knew Vinz when we were at University of Lutrum. He was... we were... Erm..."

At this point, a slightly masculine female lynx pulled out a switch blade knife and opened it, picking her claws idly with it. "And you're with the Nightwatch at all, are you, love?" she said in a voice dripping with sarcasm and suspicion. Everyone at the booth glared at him.

Elor's patience wore thin very quickly. "The knife isn't going to work," Elor said. "I should probably be standing in front of a firing squad or in the middle of a show trial about now. I was seconds from being seized by the Nightwatch because I dared question the Inakara faith in their eyes. I've already danced with death once today, twice won't make my day any worse, so you can go ahead and stab me or you can put your bloody knife away and we can talk like civilized creatures!"

The panther was breathing hard, apoplectic, and his hands were shaking slightly as he finished his tirade. No one at the booth said a word, only staring at the intensity and sincerity in his eyes. Gilyar nodded to the lynx and she quietly folded the knife, putting it away in her jacket pocket. "So sorry," she said ruefully. "We can't be too careful these days, Salaar's boys are here all the time now, trying to get the goods on us culture criminals."

"They just wait for an excuse to get us into protected airspace and pounce. I've had four just this week," Gilyar said. "Though one of them... Well, I had to do him in. He got a little too curious," The badger bowed his head, genuinely saddened by having taken another life, even if it was the life of a Nightwatch agent.

"So do you know where Vinz is?" Elor asked. "He's practically breathing down your neck," the badger replied, tapping on the table three times with a five Imperial coin.

A wolf dressed in a waiter's uniform and carrying a tray full of empty glasses came around the corner almost immediately. His eyes locked with the eyes of a very familiar panther, and his blood suddenly ran cold.

"Hello, Vinz," the panther managed to choke out somewhat awkwardly.

Vinz nodded politely. "Can I get you anything, sir?" he asked.

"A Tavellian port would be nice," Elor replied.

The wolf nodded tensely. "So it is you?" Vinz said. "I don't have time for this... I'm at work. Elor, if you really must bother me after all these years, come back when I'm not busy!"

"I'm so sorry," Elor said. The wolf nodded curtly and vanished around the corner.

"Oh... you're *that* Elor..." the lynx said knowingly. "Good luck winning him back."

CHAPTER THREE
Yes, _That_ Elor.

"No, no, no, no, no! For the last time, no! You had your chance with me, Elor, we could have fled together, but you had to put your career first, pissing away everything you love so you could be a professor just like daddy!"

The wolf huffed and fumed as he paced around a small flat built into a second-floor room in an inauspicious corner of the basecraft's shanty town. Next door a tinny sonigram recording of a fast-paced jazz dance popular before the rise of the Imperium could be heard through the thin wooden walls, and the light from a single bulb mounted in a bare fixture flickered slightly as the power from the auxiliary generators fluctuated.

Elor sat on a crate in the corner, meshing his hands together nervously. He'd followed Vinz home after he finished his shift, desperate just to find some familiar face, though knowing full well that this was how the wolf would react when they finally had a moment alone.

"Vinz, it's not what you think. I lost you and I accept that, it's over, it's done. I just need a place to stay until I can find another way..." he tried to think of what else to say, but everything else just sounded like making excuses or begging for forgiveness, and that was the last thing he wanted to do.

"Do you think you can just walk in, after this many years, and beg for a place to hang your coat after you threw me away for some empty promise?" Vinz raged. "What makes you think I wouldn't sell you to a Cylinderhead pimp looking for a little fresh meat to peddle in the back rooms at the Vixen? Felines are fifty crowns a head, what with not showing your age and all. How old's this one, then? Fifteen or thirty-five? They don't know and they don't care. You'll spend the rest of your life lifting tail to bankers and street sweepers who can't get theirs on the surface."

At this point, something ignited deep in the panther's being. He was suddenly no longer cowering, begging for forgiveness in the corner of his former lover's ramshackle flat. He stood up, his coat off and his sleeves rolled up, showing a bit more of the sinewy, well-toned form that he kept hidden beneath layers of clothing. He placed a hand beneath Vinz's chin, his touch gentle but his grip viselike in its firmness, and looked into Vinz's eyes with a strangely serene, confident look.

"Vinz, don't be ridiculous. Living in this hell hole may have changed you but I know you'd never do something like that. You're just as I remember you, defensive, arrogant, always on guard because you know you're just one harsh word from falling to pieces. I dare you to tell me I'm not dead right!"

Elor let go of the wolf's chin and backed down, strolling over and sitting on the crate once again, slumping, letting his sleeves fall back into place. He sighed heavily.

"Do you really want me to leave, Vinz?" he asked, his tone even and steady but tinged with just the right amount of disappointment.

"Would you if I said yes?" Vinz finally asked after a moment's hesitation.

"Yes," Elor said, putting on his coat and hat and reaching for his suitcases.

Vinz paused a moment. "You know this is no place to go carrying your life's possessions after lights-out, Catts," said Vinz.

The panther's ears twitched. It was an old term of endearment the wolf had called him by years before. Elor hadn't been called that in so long, and it disarmed him to hear that again.

"Don't read too much into that," the wolf said, realizing his slip of the tongue had erased any doubts that he at least cared about Elor. "Look, stay here tonight if you need to, I know some fellows who might be able to take you off my hands and get you situated tomorrow."

Elor set his luggage down, breathing a sigh of relief. "Thank you," he said.

The wolf turned and walked into a corner partitioned off from the rest of the room by a tattered canvas curtain, where his bed and a few other items sat. "I don't have a spare hammock or bedroll, you'll have to make do with what you see out there. Oh, and Elor?"

"Yes?" the panther said.

Vinz suddenly wheeled around and charged at him, a rifle with a glistening bayonet in hand. Elor stumbled backward and the wolf pointed it menacingly at his throat. "Keep your hands to yourself!" he growled.

With that, the wolf then walked briskly back to his own private corner of the room and promptly pulled the curtains shut.

Elor sat alone among his luggage. Maybe all this time in the basecraft really had changed Vinz after all; the Vinz he knew would have fainted at the sight of a gun.

He sighed softly and reached into a suitcase, rolling up one of his jackets to use as a pillow and using one of his heavier coats to cover up. Winning back Vinz's heart, it seemed, was most definitely out of the question.

Why, then, did he suddenly want it more than ever?

* * *

"Is he dead?"

Elor felt a sharp poke at his rib cage. He sensed something, a presence, a tall creature... a soldier? Prodding him with a bayonet, the sharp point digging into his ribs.

"Is he? Is he dead?"

He sensed the form of a tall canine of uncertain race, in a heavy coat, face covered with a full gas mask, eyes obscured by lifeless glass circles, prodding him, ready to stab him to make sure the job was done.

The panther jolted awake. Standing over him was a young ferret; at first, he thought, a young boy, but in only a moment he realized she was a girl in her early or mid-teens, and more than a bit of a tomboy. She had a painfully sharp piece of scrap metal in one hand and was eying him with a very confused look.

"Alrie! Stop that!" He heard Vinz's voice say.

The wolf pulled back the curtain of his private corner and stepped forward, dressed only in long underwear. "Elor... Oh... I'm so sorry. She's a good girl really, but no manners at all. Alrie! What do you say?"

"I'm sorry... cougar fella." the ferret said, wringing her hands a moment, then running off through another curtain.

"What was that all about?" Elor said.

"That's Alrie. She... sort of comes and goes as she pleases. Used to work at the Dai-Yel plant with her mother. The poor girl barely escaped the surface with her life, and she's sort of taken to me. She lives on handouts from the others in the building, mostly, and I keep the pimps and thugs away from her. Awful bastards, going after a girl so young." He shook his head.

"Why would a girl her age try to escape the surface?" asked vinz. What did she do?"

At that, the wolf paused, wondering how much he could tell someone he hadn't seen in nearly a decade. He looked back and forth suspiciously as if expecting someone to be listening in, and leaned in close as he spoke to Elor in a slightly hushed voice.

"I'll tell you this much... she seems a little odd, sometimes even comes off a bit slow... but she knows things that would amaze you. Things that got her in trouble. She's got nowhere else to run now. All of 15, and she already knows too much for her own good." The wolf shook his head sadly.

"Emperor Salaar didn't get her, and I won't let anyone else touch her. I can't tell you what she knows, Elor, but it may be the most important thing anyone in the world knows."

"I don't suppose breakfast would be too much to ask?" Elor said, changing the subject.

"Breakfast?" Vinz said. "Heh, that brings back memories. There's street vendors outside if you don't want to climb five flights of stairs to pay tourist prices. You're on your own, though."

* * *

A few minutes later, as Elor finished the sausage and chilled cider he'd bought from a cart just outside the building, he and Vinz began to discuss living arrangements.

"As you might guess, there's no rent here, we pretty much take whatever space we can, though when space is scarce there are some creatures out there who'd kill you for it. I mean that literally, Catts. I know the owner of the Vixen, Kerro Hemini. He seems to know just about every vacancy in this place. I do warn you, though... He's got a lot of ties to the Cylinderheads. If you cross him, you're dead." The wolf emphasized this last point with a nod.

"What about work?" Elor asked. "I'll need money for food and the like, obviously. I've got enough money to last a week or so but I can't hold out forever."

"Kerro can get you that too. There's always openings for waitstaff. If you're up for it, there are also plenty of opportunities in... erm... intimate services. Half our clients are males from the surface who just want a little muzzle and tail without getting shot, and as a feline... well, you do look youngish, and that's a good market."

The wolf eyed his former lover. Admittedly, Elor was still very attractive, and hadn't aged appreciably in the last nine years. Vinz himself was starting to go gray about the muzzle and paunchy around the waist- normal for a canine entering middle age but not doing him any favors for looks.

The panther knitted his eyebrows a moment. "Professor to prostitute... what a transition. No, I think I'll pass."

The wolf grinned slyly. "How long has it been anyway? Since your last fling, I mean. It must be rough going, not knowing who's into males and who's just a Nightwatch informant."

Elor sat up, adjusting his collar. "It's no business of yours how long it's been... I... Have been very busy in a professional capacity."

Vinz frowned. "Unbelievable. You've actually been celibate this entire time, haven't you?"

The panther blushed visibly under his fur. "When it's down to a paw in the pants or a bullet in the skull, you have to make some sacrifices for your own safety."

The wolf leaned forward and patted Elor between the ears. "Looks like you're nine years overdue for a good mauling, Catts," he said with a mischievous grin. "I know a fellow who's plenty experienced enough for someone like you, some sort of smallish canine, I think he said he was a jackal. I'll let him know you're here."

Elor cleared his throat. "Thank you, I think I'll look on my own. So, until I find a place of my own, can I keep my things here?" he said, motioning to his suitcases.

"You're welcome to keep your things here... and yourself too, if you like," Vinz said. "Sorry about last night, it was just... I was... not having a good night." The wolf seemed to avert his eyes, as if trying to avoid the consequences of contact.

"Never mind," said Elor knowingly, lowering his gaze to ease Vinz's worries. "I really shouldn't have imposed on you like this."

"No, no, really... You probably did the wise thing, this is no place for a newcomer. I had some rough times when I got here, robbed twice, once I even got shot and nearly died." The wolf lifted his shirt, revealing a slightly rounder but still well-formed chest and belly, with one small circular scar just below the ribcage. "A 9mm round through the spleen really hurts, Elor. I learned that the hard way and it's still in there somewhere to remind me when the weather gets cold."

Elor winced at the thought. "So, when do we speak to Kerro?" the panther asked, anxious to begin his new life.

"I'll probably speak to him tonight, I work evenings at the Vixen," Vinz replied. "I need to go out and get some errands done today, and probably won't be home until after work. You should probably stay here... I wouldn't recommend exploring too much on your own until you're better known, they might think you're with the Nightwatch. There's a television set in my room, along with some books... there's even one or two all-male magazines somewhere around here. Just put everything back where you found it and don't make a mess. Oh, yes, and if you have to use the pot, use that steel bucket in the corner. There's a waste grate behind the building, empty the bucket there when you're done."

Vinz left, and Elor made for the wolf's little corner of the flat without hesitation, pulling aside the curtain. There, in the small space, was a bed laying atop crates that were filled with books and papers, a small shelf with more books and a few trinkets, a television set, and a very familiar box marked with a light blue feather in a gold ring... Elor chuckled when he saw it, knowing full well that the wolf's taste in adult toys was very interesting and that there may be some new items to use some other time when Vinz was out.

The television set, a small console unit that was barely more than a radio with a small picture tube on top, was wired up in a way Elor had never seen. Rather than an antenna on top, there was a small box with a wire running into the wall. He turned it on and found that rather than having to tune it, it picked up the channel clearly. A news program was playing, with footage of the airport outside Highridge. Off screen, an anchor's voice, dripping with glib and drama, practically vomited out the accompanying story as music played in the background.

"Authorities with the Nightwatch and MTTS are investigating the escape of seditionist professor Elor Kaya. Nightwatch agents had been sent to apprehend the suspect but were just shy of capturing this dangerous fugitive. He was last seen on an airliner bound for Archer's Cove and is believed to have taken refuge on Basecraft Cirrostratus, and is believed to have boarded using falsified travel papers."

Elor couldn't believe this. He had been prepared to forge the correct documents, but the MTTS field office in Highridge had issued those papers without hesitation because he was not yet in their files as a flight risk. Now they were denying it to save face.

"Kaya joins a long list of other fugitives believed to be somewhere on the basecraft, but as yet Emperor Salaar has decided mercifully to grant them asylum there."

They then showed the emperor himself, addressing the press with a wide array of microphones before him, the scene occasionally whited out by photographers' flash bulbs.

"Our society cannot function without law, and law must function within limits," he blustered. "The criminals we believe live within the belly of the various basecraft have, unfortunately, found the limits of our laws and exploited them. The air space these ships travel in is international, and as yet we are bound by our laws and treaties. However, I want every single creature, lawful and outlaw alike, to know that my patience is limited. The day is coming, very, very soon, when we will throw off the chains of international treaties and do what must be done. We will take action and bring these criminals to justice, and it will be done soon, and without warning."

The blustering, boastful propaganda continued on and on. Elor lost his patience with the broadcast relatively quickly and turned the channel.

After some searching, he found another channel playing an old film called "Rise, Modern Creature," one he was surprised to see because it was banned in the Imperium for its references to evolution. At first he thought it might be an errant signal from Lycocia, but then realized that such a signal would probably be fuzzy and indistinct if it could travel this far to begin with. Elor then realized that the wire in the back of the television must have been some sort of internal feed to a television network within the basecraft.

"Remarkable!" he said with a surprised chuckle. Perhaps Salaar's investments in developing communications had done some good after all.

Elor sat on the bed and watched the film, letting himself relax for the first time in a very, very long time.

He was rudely awakened by the blaze of artificial light that came as the curtain was pulled aside. At first Elor jumped, thinking it was the Nightwatch, but his terror turned to relief and then annoyance when he noticed that it was Vinz, with a fox who looked to be some years younger than himself, both of them wearing little more than a pair of plain linen trunks that were distinctly tented at the front.

The panther just looked the two over and sighed. "I'll leave you two be," he said, and shuffled out toward the Cunning Little

Vixen. Seeing Vinz with a new date was hardly the best thing that could happen to him so soon after arriving on the Cirrostratus. This occasion called for a strong one.

"Who was that?" the fox asked Vinz.

"Someone from long ago on the surface. Had some trouble with the law and needed a place to stay," the wolf replied.

"He's not one of your new tricks, is he?" the fox said, folding back his ears slightly.

Vinz sighed. "No, his name's Elor. We were together years ago, but that's dead."

"Oh, *that* Elor," the fox replied.

Vinz chuckled. "Right, nothing between us. It's still you I want, foxy."

With that Vinz slid a hand into the waist of the fox's linen shorts, a gesture that was greeted by a warm and approving moan. "Now where were we?"

In seconds both were down to nothing but their fur, the fox lying on top of the wolf, each nuzzling the other warmly. "So, what does my wuffy want tonight, hmm?" the fox said, sitting up and grinding his rear against Vinz's firming maleness. "Mmmf... that would be good," said Vinz.

Instinctively, the fox reached for a tube of lotion kept near the wolf's bed- hardly the best lubricant but it did the job. He rubbed a generous amount under his tail, then along Vinz's exposed, trembling shaft.

He leaned forward and kissed the wolf deeply on the muzzle, Vinz growling softly and returning the kiss with full tongue. The fox reached back to stroke his lover's flesh for just a moment, then slowly, delicately, he sat up and lowered himself on the larger canine's flesh.

"Mmmf... I love it when you do that," said Vinz, grabbing the fox's hips and thrusting upward slightly. In only moments, instinct took over and the fox began to ride Vinz's shaft furiously up and down.

Suddenly, the fox stopped, dismounted, then crouched on the bed, his thick bushy tail lifted. Vinz grinned, getting up and mounting his lover from behind with little hesitation. The fox squealed slightly as Vinz roughly entered him, leaning forward and growling slightly as he plunged in and out with wild abandon.

He let out a howl as his knot seized within the smaller canid's body, a climax instantly rippling throughout his form. The fox responded with a higher-pitched but equally passionate howl as a strong hand reached under him and squeezed his knot tightly, setting him off almost instantaneously.

The fox panted. "Do you... think we woke the neighbors?" he said. "Six months together and we haven't woken them yet," Vinz replied, settling on top of his lover and letting out a deep sigh of satisfaction.

"Say Vinz," said the fox, "You know if you still had feelings for the cougar, I'd be fine with it, right? I'm not the jealous type."

Vinz let out a different sort of sigh. "Just let it be, Laz. Let it be," he said. "That's over and done, I'm through searching. It's you I want now."

Laz sighed. "This isn't because of the whole 'I'm getting old' thing, is it? Vinz, you don't look near as bad as you could. It won't hurt you to try your luck to make sure you've got the right fellow, and I won't hold it against you. I'll still be here."

Vinz leaned in and gave the scruff of Laz's neck a playful nip. "But what if I don't want to keep looking, foxy?" He ground his still-locked shaft deep into the fox's body, eliciting a moan from his handsome lover.

"You've made your case," said Laz, reaching to give Vinz's chin a loving scratch.

Vinz sighed and settled atop Laz. How many times had he made that case before? It wasn't all in his head, he was getting old, and soon it would be impossible to find a good date. When he'd met Laz, the former mechanic who survived on odd jobs within the shanty town, he knew he had a good thing and didn't want to let it go.

No one, no matter how much they had meant to him in the past, would ever come between him and Laz. Ever.

CHAPTER FOUR
An Offer He Can't Refuse

The sound of a familiar tune greeted Elor's ears as the panther approached the Cunning Little Vixen, a tune that had been outlawed long ago back on the surface. He didn't even recall its title or the lyrics, only the rollicking piano and loud, almost lascivious blast of muted brass that made the communications and culture ministers declare it a bad influence on youth.

Inside, the bar was just as busy as it had been the night before, and with the usual crowd in attendance. If not for the large, neon minimalist clock on the back wall Elor might have sworn it was the same time of night. But The Vixen never slept, and neither, it seemed, did most of its regular customers.

He walked cautiously past the bar in front where the Cylinderheads sat, sucking down shot after shot of their own smuggled libations. He hoped to make it to the restaurant and club area just a short distance away without attracting too much attention, but it was no use; one of them happened to notice him.

"You look like you could use some protection, sir," said a coyote with a twisted grin and a huge hideous scar running in a crescent from his forehead to behind his right ear. He wore only jeans, boots, an oil-stained white undershirt, and fingerless gloves.

Elor froze, pinning back his ears. This fellow was a good bit smaller than himself, but looked to be a formidable fighter who wasn't afraid to come out of a scuffle with a scar or two. The panther's eyes darted about, looking for a way out.

"I got some merchandise here in this trunk that might interest you," the coyote said with a sneer.

With that,he pulled a large old trunk from under the bar

and whipped it open. Inside, a full array of every sort of gun imaginable could be seen. Laying across the jumbled heap was one very large and particularly frightening gun with a steel belt of high-caliber ammunition feeding into its receiver.

The coyote reached in and pulled out a short-barreled rifle with a drum magazine and handed it to Elor. "Gyram GK-12 machine gun. Like new. Got it from a Lycocian mob boss, he sure didn't need it no more."

The remark drew knowing laughs from the rest of the sordid crowd at the bar. "Takes an 11mm rimless pistol round, that magazine holds about 50 of 'em, though one squeeze on that trigger and you'll empty the whole thing into someone's skull. I can make you a nice deal on this 'un, 250 Crowns and it's yours, I'll even throw in the bullets."

Elor was not impressed. "I think some other time. I really can't afford that right now," he said dryly.

The coyote reached in and pulled out a big, primitive-looking revolver that looked like something he'd seen the police carrying when he was just a boy. "How about this 'un, then? This is a classic, a Binega Five. Holds five 9mm rounds, very good at close range, I can sell it to you for 50 Crowns."

Elor tried to make his way toward the entrance to the club, backing toward the doorway. "Erm... no, I think some other time perhaps..."

He felt a broad hand on his shoulder and looked behind him, seeing only a mountain of dark brown fur and cloth. Looking up he found himself staring at a massive bear wearing a leather vest and a pilot's cap. "He wants to sell you a weapon, cat, that's an honor, he doesn't make his offers to everyone. I think you'd better show him some respect and buy something."

The figures who had previously been sitting at the bar now gathered around him, eying him menacingly. Elor was not sure what to do; he'd left all but five crowns at Vinz's place, and that five was just enough to buy a few drinks and maybe some food if he felt like it later.

Suddenly a door at the back of the room opened. A serious-looking stoat about Elor's age strode out, wearing a smart-looking pinstripe suit bedecked with diamond-studded buttons and cufflinks. He held his position and expression, and spoke in a calm, metered tone with a Lycocian accent. "Leave him alone, Klarn. Remember our agreement, these high-pressure sales shenanigans are bad for business, that's bad for me and it's bad for you because if business is bad, I can't buy your whiskey."

The coyote's demeanor changed instantly. "We're just tryin' to squeeze a few more crowns out, sell a few guns, nothing wrong with that," he said, trying to sound apologetic.

"You can sell guns all you like, but within these walls, when the customer says no, that means no. Anyway, this guy doesn't look like an idiot. I think he'll buy something from you, sooner or later." With that the stoat gave Elor a long, knowing stare.

Elor nodded, feeling very uneasy. "Indeed I will," he said.

"Now be nice to our customers! If you wanna fuck with someone, take it outside. You got it?" the stoat demanded. There was a general murmur of agreement and lots of nodding as the Cylinderheads went back to minding their own business, the trunk full of weapons being slid out of view once again.

"Sorry," the bear said to both of them, lifting the brim of his flight cap respectfully before shuffling back to a table in the corner of the bar.

The stoat then walked up to Elor. Short though he was, he carried himself like a tall creature in every way. He commanded attention, and had a certain air of roguish authority about him. Elor knew him instantly for what he was: a prince of thieves, in the flesh.

"I can't tell you how sorry I am," he said. "These guys just don't know how to treat a guest. I'm Kerro Hemini, owner of this here fine establishment. If there's any way I can make it up to you, please, do say so."

The panther nodded. "Actually, I was looking for you. I just arrived here, last night..."

The stoat raised his hand "Oh, I see where this is headed. Why don't we talk about this in my office? Right this way, sir, right this way."

With that the stoat turned and walked through the discreet

door at the back of the room he had entered by. Elor followed, not sure what to expect. To his surprise, the door had concealed a corridor built into the back of the basecraft itself. The two walked down the dimly-lit corridor toward a steel ladder some meters ahead, then climbed down one level.

They were now at the sixth sublevel, a part of the ship typically off-limits to the public. They walked down a similar corridor until they were in a vast, near-empty hold with a few shipping crates and miscellaneous items.

At first Elor was surprised by the vastness of his surroundings, but then realized that this hold had the exact dimensions of the massive hold that contained the shanty town above them.

"The shipping companies use this as storage, either waiting for a foreign freight company to pick up an item or waiting for customs to approve import papers. Our little city was never meant to exist, the operators of the basecraft only agreed to it after I convinced them it'd make them a few extra crowns by bringing the tourists in," Kerro explained.

They walked to one of the near corners of the hold, where one enormous shipping crate sat marked *Pyron GP2943 Aero Engine, Product of Lycocia*. Kerro opened a discreet door in its side and stepped into it.

There were few offices back on the surface this plush- or this vulgar. Inside the crate was a suite whose decor ranged from high-class executive furniture to the tawdry velvet and tinsel one would expect of a brothel from Lycocia's desert frontier. The walls were covered in a bright red lace-patterned wallpaper, with pictures of females of various species in various states of undress framed haphazardly all over them. The room was lit by a set of otherwise-plain lamps bedecked in red organdy shades with black feather boas trimming their edges. Everything from the deep-pile burgundy carpet to the gold-painted pressed-tin ceiling was immaculately clean, and in the midst of it all sat a massive neoclassical desk with two wing-backed chairs on either side of it. Perched on the desk were only a writing pad, a pen in its inkwell, and a surprisingly plain black plastic telephone, its rotary dial tarnished from heavy use.

The stoat sat behind the desk, and motioned for Elor to take a seat. "First of all, let me be blunt, I know why you're here and no, I can't just give you a job," he said, folding his hands in front of him on the desk as Elor took his seat.

"I understand, sir," Elor said. "I understand my background doesn't qualify me very well for work in a jazz and whiskey bar..."

"Fuck your background," Kerro said flatly, "I mean right now I've got everyone I need. Oh, I grant you, rate of attrition is normally high, as they say in the business world."

The stoat reached into a humidor under the desk and took out a cigar, biting off the end and placing it in his mouth, lighting it nonchalantly. "Trouble is, we've been stable the last few months. No one's left and no one's gone missing or dead. Good for business, bad for you. Now let's get down to why we're here. I try to run a clean outfit... clean as I can in my racket. I'm not going to sit by while those thugs harass my clients, even if they do provide me with certain merchandise. So between you and me, I'll give you something nice within reason if you'll kindly forget about your little run-in with the Cylinderheads. Just no jobs, can't help you there."

The stoat flicked ashes from his cigar into a brass ashtray as Elor thought about the proposition. "How about a bottle of Tavel Regal brandy, vintage '98?" Elor said.

"Don't lets be greedy, now! I said within reason!" Kerro replied, fully aware that such spirits fetched about 400 crowns on the black market.

"Well, then... One of those cigars and... a few crowns to get me through."

The stoat reached into his humidor and produced a full, unopened box of the same fine cigars from under his desk. "Why take just one? I can't smoke all of these. Consider the cigars on the house. But trust me, if I were you I'd buy a GK-12. Here..."

He reached into his pocket and pulled out seven 50 crown notes and a piece of paper. He scrawled a name on a piece of paper. "This guy can sell one to you for 150, that gives you a little extra to spare for whatever. He lives just around the corner from here, in an old insulated railway container. Just one thing... If I give you this money, you owe me a favor, and when I'm owed a favor I always collect."

He made the last of these terms with a menacing grin and leaned forward.

Elor kept his composure, though he was rather uneasy about what these terms entailed. "What favor would I owe you?" he said,, shifting in his seat a bit but otherwise not flustered.

"There's a Nightwatch agent who's been trying to get the dirt on my clients," the stoat replied. "He's been asking some questions that hit a little too close."

With that Kerro produced a blurry photograph from one of his desk drawers. It was just clear enough to make out the form of an otter in the signature black overcoat and bowler hat of a Nightwatch agent. "I want him dead. He's been harassing my suppliers looking for tips on a fugitive, and if my suppliers get scared and withdraw, that's bad for business. You in?"

Elor thought about it for a moment. A Nightwatch agent was bad news, but was it really right to agree to kill one in cold blood? Then again, 350 crowns with 200 left for food and necessities was not something he could afford to turn down.

The moral dilemma seemed somewhat less black and white when it was purely a question of survival. Suddenly it was more like a predator and its prey; this agent would die, and Elor would live. Still, the whole thing didn't sit right with him. But what of the consequences if he said no? Did he really want to risk that?

Elor nodded, standing and extending his hand. "I'm in," he said, a distinctive lump in his throat.

"Do this for me and I might throw in a bit more when you've done the job," Kerro said, taking Elor's hand and giving it a firm shake.

Elor shuddered a bit at the prospect of being a career killer. "We shall see," he said, sliding the money into his vest pocket and stepping toward the door. "Thank you, Mr. Hemini. If you'll excuse me I was just on my way to have a few drinks. It's been a hard week for me."

"You're welcome at the Vixen any time. And hey, do this for

me and I'm Kerro to you from that day on," the stoat said. "By the way, I never did get your name."

"Profes... I mean, Elor Kaya, the title is useless now."

"Oh... you're *that* Elor," the stoat said.

Elor flattened his ears a bit; it had only been said a few times but he was already getting tired of hearing it. Just what had Vinz been saying about him, anyway?

"Just one thing," Elor said as he made his way to the door, "Why would a gang of ruthless thugs sell weapons that can be used against them?"

Kerro just laughed. "Do you really think anyone's going to actually shoot a Cylinderhead? You're a class act, kid, I'll see ya around!"

Elor returned to the apartment some time later, after a few drinks and a plate of potatoes and bacon from a street vendor. Vinz had left, and the lights outside the apartment had begun to dim as the day faded on. In Vinz's corner he could make out a musky smell that left little doubt that the wolf and the fox had enjoyed themselves thoroughly.

The panther sat back and lit one of the cigars, somewhat envious of the wolf's luck. Maybe Vinz's offer to introduce him to some of Kerro's escorts wasn't such a bad idea.

BASECRAFT CIRROSTRATUS

CHAPTER FIVE
Contract Killings and Other Humdrum Chores

"You did *what?!?*"

Vinz could not, for the life of him, believe that Elor had been so stupid. In just one day in the holds of this basecraft, the panther had sealed his fate.

"There's no work, I only had about forty crowns left, and he'd just saved me from a bad run-in with the Cylinderheads, Vinz, it's not like I could just say no." The panther's ears were back, tail twitching with pronounced agitation.

"Catts, you don't understand. Right now they won't come after you because you're just a garden variety offender. They can't afford come after you, there are so many dissidents and deviants here that we're not worth the red tape. But if you kill a Nightwatch agent, they won't even bother with the red tape. They'll target you, and everyone around you, and that means I'd be in danger too, and everyone around me." The wolf's voice was strained and cracked by exasperation; it was the sort of frustration colored with dismay one would expect in hearing someone close to them had made a fatal decision.

"Then maybe I should give the money back," Elor replied. "If I don't have his money, I don't owe him anything, do I?"

"It's not that simple, Catts. When Kerro gets your word, he holds you to it. If you back out now, he'll pretend it doesn't bother him, then about five Cylinderheads will grab you and toss you over the edge of the flight deck. If you don't believe me, ask anyone about Gwyral Magor." The wolf shuddered slightly thinking of the episode, though he did not elaborate.

"Then supposing I never find this agent?" Elor asked.

"If you never find him, we'll never find your body," Vinz replied.

Elor sat down in the corner of the room. He let out a loud, long sight, then a nervous chuckle. "I always knew it would end this way, Vinz. The big dilemma. Damned if I do, damned if I don't."

He turned and looked Vinz straight in the eyes in a way he hadn't in many, many years. "I can't draw you into the line of fire, though. I'll be on my way tonight while you're at work, and I'll find some other corner of this hold to hide in."

"Farewell," said Vinz, pulling aside the curtain for privacy as he undressed for the evening- and to hide the fact that he was on the verge of tears.

Almost as soon as Vinz had stepped out of sight, there was a frantic knock at the door. Elor hesitated, but at the muffled sound of a frantic young voice on the other side, quickly changed his mind. He opened the door and in stumbled Alrie, sweaty, her eyes filled with fear.

"What is it?" Elor asked.

"Close the door!" Alrie shouted, darting into Vinz's curtained-off corner.

The wolf was startled to see Alrie, and was just about to ask her to leave when he heard the door being kicked open violently. "Where is she?" a voice shouted. Vinz peered out to see an otter in a black bowler hat and his heart sank. He didn't hear the distinct click behind him.

The otter looked surprised and drew a Nightwatch issue pistol, but dropped in a spray of crimson before he could fire.

Vinz wheeled around to see Elor holding his rifle, the barrel smoking. Alrie clung to Vinz's leg in absolute terror, a soft whimpering sob escaping her as she saw what had just happened.

Elor was breathing hard as he dropped the rifle from his sweaty palms. It landed with a loud clatter on the wooden floor. He swallowed, then turned slowly, looking at Vinz with a dazed expression. "That was him," he said in a quiet voice.

Vinz tore the curtain from his corner of the room free of its hanging points, gathering it up in his hands and walking over to the body. "Come on, if we get rid of this we may still have a chance," the wolf said.

"Didn't anyone hear that? I just fired a rifle for Ovego's sake!" Elor replied, his hands still trembling.

"Happens about once a week in these flats, that's why I bought the damn thing," Vinz said. "Now come on! They're bound to notice he's missing."

"What about Alrie?" the panther asked, the terrified young ferret still huddling close to Vinz.

"She should be safe here," Vinz said, tearing the pistol from the otter's stiff hand and handing it to Alrie. "She's from a rough part of Northarbour. She'll know what to do if anyone gives her trouble."

Vinz made to wrap up the body, but Elor stopped him. "Wait..." He reached into the otter's pockets, pulling out their contents. A small pocket knife, about 23 Crowns in coins and notes, a vacation photo that he respectfully placed back in his pocket... where was it? Then he found what he was looking for in one of the inner pockets of the otter's coat. A polished steel badge in the shape of a heraldic shield glinted in his hand, with the otter's name and serial number engraved on it.

"Agent Hollax, number SP7698912," Elor read aloud. Vinz gave him a puzzled look.

"Kerro will want to see this," he explained.

"We can't risk him being found in uniform," Vinz said, and began stripping the body of its clothes. "We'll burn these, there's a rubbish chute that leads to a furnace not far from here.".

Elor hesitated, wanting to at least grant the agent some dignity in death, but with a sigh he threw his hands up and began helping Vinz. With the bloody clothes now in a separate pile, they wrapped the agent's body and carried it quickly out the door.

* * *

Some distance away, a Star Javelin interceptor roared along through the darkening sky. Its pilot, an otter about 26 years of age, looked at his fuel gage and shook his head in dismay. He was a long way from the flight plan and he knew it, and the Star Javelin, a sleek, powerful single-engined fighter and light bomber, was not known for its range... nor for its glide angle upon losing power.

I can't go back to Tartús, though. I can't keep bombing civilians, he thought to himself. The mountainous, semi-autonomous region of Tartús some distance to the north and east of the former Occidentania was one of the few cells of resistance to the Great Wolven Imperium, and Emperor Salaar's military apparatus was well-focused on softening them up.

The otter knew the Basecraft Cirrostratus had to be near, but could not risk being seen landing on it. He knew as soon as he found the basecraft, he had to swing upward as hard as he could, bail out, and hope that he could aim his clumsy, round service issue parachute well enough to land on its deck. In his survival pack was an inflatable raft, but it wouldn't be much use to him; if he couldn't land on the deck of the Cirrostratus his survival would depend on being picked up by sailors who would not return him to a GWI port. On the other hand, his desertion and refusal to carry out orders- namely to bomb an orphanage as a measure to instill fear in the Tartussian resistance- had already sealed his fate. He could die now with the off chance of surviving, or he could die later with no chance at all.

The dense fog and cloud cover blotted the full moon from view, giving poor visibility. Meanwhile, the plane's engine was beginning to cough and sputter as it reached the dregs of its main fuel tank. He pulled the lever opening the small reserve tank- enough to buy him about ten more minutes- and scanned the sky intently.

Five minutes passed. Six. Seven. Eight... Then just as the ninth minute was looming, he saw the flashing light of the Cirrostratus' aft beacon. He opened the throttle wide and roared toward it, then nosed up hard, climbing nearly a kilometer above and slightly to one side of the craft so as not to have the unpiloted plane crash into the ship. He pulled the quick release on his safety harness and jammed the release lever for the canopy open. The wind rushing by at 400 kilometers per hour hit his face with a frightening force, one he had not been prepared for. He nosed the plane forward into a downward arc and felt himself rise, weightless from the cockpit. He pushed away with his feet and was at last free of the doomed craft.

He reached to open his chute, fumbling a moment, then pulling the cord. He was jolted hard as the envelope of synthetic fibers caught the air above him and slowed his descent, the plane's vertical stabilizer missing him by only a hair's breadth.

He felt a stinging pain and reached up to touch his face. He winced, then pulled back his hand, just barely able to make out the blood that covered his gloved palm. He was lucky a nosebleed and a possible broken nose was all he'd gotten from such a risky maneuver.

Using what little control he had over the clumsy round chute, the otter began trying as well as he could to hit the deck of the Cirrostratus, watching as his fighter plunged out of sight into the inky blackness below.

* * *

Meanwhile, far below, Elor and Vinz arrived at the end of a narrow corridor tucked away just behind a block of flats on the edge of the hold. At its end, a heavy steel door sat, its latch held shut by a screw-driven spring mechanism.

"They use these hatches for servicing the craft when she's drydocked," the wolf explained. "Though... well, we're not the first to use them this way."

Vinz turned a large wheel on the heavy steel hatch, turning the screw to engage the springs. The screw finally caught and the spring latch slid open with a loud bang. He pushed the door open, a cold night breeze blowing into the corridor.

Without further ado, he and Elor hoisted the slain agent's remains forward, shoving them out into the night.

Vinz made to close the hatch, but then stopped. "What is

it?" Elor asked.

"Take a look," Vinz replied and pointed toward a faint white shape, barely visible in the cloud-blotted moonlight. The form got closer and closer, and Elor began to make out the vague shape of a parachute and its user.

"He's aiming for the ship, this doesn't look good, though. I don't think he'll make it," Vinz said grimly.

"Isn't there a way? There has to be something to catch him," Elor said.

"A fishing boat, maybe," Vinz replied.

"A fishing boat? Supposing there aren't any?" Elor replied, sounding upset.

"We can't just reach out there and grab him! Look, he's already going below the level of this doorway," the wolf said. "You've seen death before... it's never easy, but it's true, the poor fellow won't make it, and I can't make that any better."

Elor didn't hear this last remark. He was already searching the corridor for something- anything- that could work. He suddenly saw something he hadn't thought of before, a pulley just outside the doorway on a small jib, used to moor the ship in place. The end of the cable stretched over it was latched conveniently to the side of the ship so that a worker could unlatch it from within.

Without saying a word, he unlatched the line, threw the lever that made the winch go slack, hastily hooked the end over the line to create a lasso, then threw it downward toward the quickly-falling pilot.

The lasso missed. Elor swung the line from side to side, letting our more slack as quickly as he could, hoping the poor fellow would be able to grab it.

He finally reached the end of the line, and it swayed in he breeze. Only a few brief moments had passed, but it seemed like an eternity, and the line still held slack. Elor sighed softly, his ears sagging as he let go of the line.

Just then, the line snapped taut and begin to swing sharply outward with the wind.

* * *

Far below, the otter clung to the line with all his might. The thin strand of steel cable, stretching several hundred meters from the basecraft far above, was his last hope. Holding himself up with one hand, he unlatched the lassoed end and hooked the latch to his harness.

Safe, if not comfortable, he cut his chute loose. The soft white half-sphere drifted out and then down, plummeting toward the ocean looking like a dying jellyfish.

Now it was time to wait and see if whoever had thrown him that line was going to reel him in, or let him die of exposure while dangling from a basecraft.

He began to feel himself lose consciousness as he dangled perilously, far below the enormous basecraft, the moan of the wind and the drone of the craft's massive compound radial engines the only sound.

* * *

"Give me a hand, will you?" Elor shouted as he began to turn the heavy crank that operated the winch. It was obviously not made to use under these conditions, and almost certainly needed two creatures to turn it efficiently.

Vinz said nothing, instead flipping a small switch on the wall next to him. A soft whir of machinery could be heard and the winch began turning on its own, the hand crank suddenly going slack in Elor's hand. "Always one to do things the hard way, weren't you, Catts?" he said.

Elor wanted to tell Vinz exactly what he thought of that remark, but was preoccupied with the rescue. He looked down to see who- or what- was on the end of the line.

At last a faint shape came into view. He was a young otter, dressed in a military issue flight suit. A patch on his right shoulder could be seen, indicating he was a lieutenant in the Imperial Air Force. He hung there limply, and Elor couldn't be sure if he was even alive, let alone conscious.

Finally the long ascent was over, and Vinz and Elor pulled

the unfortunate pilot into the corridor, unlatching the cable from his harness. Elor took care to latch the cable back exactly as they found it.

Vinz shut the hatch, turning the wheel in the opposite direction. The heavy latch slid back in place, sealing the heavy steel door with a loud bang. The wolf then turned his attention toward Elor and the pilot.

Elor, meanwhile, leaned over the pilot, looking him over carefully. "He's alive, some minor injuries, but he's in a bit of a daze," the panther said, looking over his charge worriedly.

"Let's take him home, maybe he can tell us something once he's warmed up," Vinz said.

The two lifted him up, each of them supporting him under one arm. The otter at first didn't try to stand, but as they walked down the corridor he did step with them, supporting himself feebly on his short legs.

"No worries, you'll be fine in a moment," said Vinz, hoping that the dazed otter would believe him. The otter could only nod slowly as they pulled him through the shanty town to Vinz's apartment, his swaying tail the only indication that he was not entirely at ease.

CHAPTER SIX
Alibis Fall From the Skies

"Murder!"

A shot rang out, and Vinz and Elor ducked, pulling the pilot with them. They could hear the whiz of the bullet and its splintering impact with the wooden wall behind them. "Murder! You won't take me alive! Death to Salaar!" Alrie shouted, aiming the pistol for a second shot.

"Alrie! Stop, enough! He's not an agent," said Vinz. Elor wrestled the gun out of Alrie's hand; the ferret resisted for a moment, but loosened her grip and let him take it, giving him a dirty look.

They laid the pilot out on Vinz's bed, putting a pillow and a spare sheet in a tight roll under his head while covering him with a warm fleece blanket. "Let's give him a moment to rest," Elor said. "I think he'll be fine."

"A bit of luck, don't you think? We dispose of one otter and another just falls out of the sky," Vinz said, turning his attention to wiping up the blood from the deceased Nightwatch agent.

"Not sure how that's to our advantage," the panther said. "Kerro might see him and think I haven't done my job, meanwhile the other agents on the basecraft will know for certain it's not him."

"I still think he can be of some use," Vinz replied. "There'll be no harm in telling Kerro he's here, he's a right bastard but he'll never cooperate with the Nightwatch."

The semiconscious pilot moaned, turning his head and reaching a hand to rub it. He opened his eyes, still looking dazed.

"Are you alright?" asked Vinz. "Lucky we were there, you'd be waiting for a boat that would never come if we'd been a moment later."

"Where am I?" the pilot asked in a hoarse voice.

"You're inside the Basecraft Cirrostratus," Elor replied.

"Obviously not in the luxury suite. Are you crew?" the otter asked.

"No, only a couple unfortunates who can't go back to the surface," Vinz said.

"I've either come to the right place or I'm delirious and half-dead," the otter replied.

"So... who are you anyway?" Elor asked.

At this the otter slowly sat up, looking him in the eye. "Lt. Bram Malga, 103rd Interceptor Wing, serial IG49453," he replied in a clipped, mechanical manner. He then lay back down, rubbing his head as it throbbed brutally.

"You're no prisoner, mate, no need to give us the name-rank-serial business," Vinz said flatly.

At that the otter sighed. "Old habits die hard, don't they? I suppose the rank means nothing. I'm not going back to the front. If Salaar wants to drop bombs on innocent civilians he can drop them himself. I don't care if they're Tartussians, I'm not going to bomb a bloody orphanage."

"A deserter?" Vinz said.

"You don't miss a thing, do you?" Bram replied.

"You look young for an officer," Elor said. "Go through an officer training program?"

"No," said Bram, "Earned my way from enlistment. I'm 26, been in the service a decade. I lied about my age to get in. Funny thing is when they found out I wasn't 18 all I got was a tongue lashing," Bram said.

"That's still impressive, to make it to lieutenant from enlisted before 30," said Vinz. "My father was 40 before he received his stripes."

"Anyone I know?" Bram asked.

"I doubt it. My father died in an automobile accident just a year before Emperor Salaar came to power. Lucky for him, I suppose," Vinz said grimly.

Bram tried to sit up one more time, but once again had to lay back, still rubbing his throbbing head. "I still don't feel well. I need some rest. I am pretty hungry too, but I think I can wait," he said, stretching out and closing his eyes.

"I think we could all use a good night's rest," Elor said. "Vinz, have anywhere you'd prefer to sleep?"

"I think I can manage," Vinz said, pulling out a couple of spare blankets and pillows from a trunk near his bed, taking one of each and handing the rest to Elor.

"Where were these when I got here?" Elor said, a bit indignant.

"Didn't want you to get too comfortable last night, but it seems with things as they are our lots are thrown in together whether we like it or not," the wolf replied. "I'm guilty by association now... may as well make the best of it."

The two settled down, each in their own corners of the room, and began to relax, Vinz stretched out on the wooden floor and Elor propping himself up partially on his suitcases.

"So tell me about Alrie," said Elor, noticing the ferret had left the room. "Why does she always come to you when there's trouble?"

Vinz sighed. "No telling how she did it, but somehow she escaped from the Dai-Yel factory... during regular work hours, at that. It was about four months ago, she arrived here, knew nothing of the place. Funny, coming from the poor ghettos of Lutrum, she should have been prepared, but she honestly thought this'd be some kind of promised land. When I found her she had about four surface dwellers hitting her up for certain... favors. Nearly lost my job for what I did to that lot."

Elor nodded. "So she takes to you as a sort of protector?" he asked.

"Somewhat," said Vinz, "though it's not that simple. Still comes and goes as she pleases, has plenty of others she gets food and shelter from, and I've seen her in a fight; she's no weakling. I think she just thinks of me as a sort of brother figure, is all."

"So why was the same Nightwatch agent that Kerro wanted dead after Alrie?" Elor asked. "What is it about her, anyway? You said she knew something, didn't you?"

Vinz shifted uncomfortably, turning away from Elor. "Never mind, maybe I'll explain tomorrow," he said. "In the mean time try to get some rest, we don't know what tomorrow is going to bring."

All three creatures slept soundly, thoroughly exhausted after a long, terrifying day that had just set everything on its ear.

*   *   *

Word circulated quickly at Nightwatch headquarters: Agent Hollax had been seen late the previous evening, being supported by a wolf and a panther, dead drunk. The sighting had been phoned in by an informer living within the holds of the basecraft, posing as an insane drifter. Agent Hollax had then failed to report for duty the next day.

Not that it was truly like Agent Hollax to do this; he was an experienced and trusted agent, totally devoted to his job and never once cited for misconduct. He had brought in at least three dozen known offenders in his five year career, and had shown himself to be a competent and capable operative in the field.

At the time of the incident, he was working on two very important cases. One involved a possible Cylinderhead smuggling ring in Foxport, and the other involved a young fugitive named Alrie Wenna. Both trails had led him to the Basecraft Cirrostratus, where he was last seen.

The Nightwatch director, an older canine of uncertain race, sat at his desk frowning at the report, straightening his horn-rimmed spectacles. Behind him a small electric fan hummed away next to the window. Slivers of daylight filtered in through the broad aluminum blinds, supplemented by a single, bare bulb in a fixture on the ceiling in the sparsely-furnished office.

Standing in the doorway, one hand on the knob of a frosted-glass door, stood a young gray fox in a white shirt and neatly-creased black trousers held up with dark red braces. He looked worried... it seemed it was always his job to be the bearer of bad news as a junior agent.

"Come in," said the director. The fox nodded, then opened

the door. He said nothing as he handed the director a report from the field office in Archer's Cove, then stood back, tail tucked and ears folded.

The director paid no attention to his nervous underling for the time being. He read through the report, frowning more and more as he read the details of Agent Hollax's apparent failure and misconduct.

He turned to a well-used typewriter, an archaic sort with round, projecting keys and long polished nickel handles on the return levers, and typed out a letter with quick, deliberate strokes of his short fingers.

He pulled the paper out rather roughly, creasing it slightly as the rollers of the typewriter grabbed it, then pulled the tab on his pen, filling the reservoir and signing the letter with a single motion. He held the letter out for the junior agent.

"Pass this to my secretary, be sure to mention I want all field offices alerted of my decision. I want Agent Hollax relieved of his duties and a warrant issued for his immediate arrest."

"Yes sir," the young agent said, turning to leave, his black-striped tail twitching nervously.

"Oh, and one more thing?" the director said.

"Yes sir?" he said, turning an ear.

"Calm down! You'll never make it to field agent unless you can show a bit of confidence. If you don't want to be a paper pusher for the rest of your career, you need to be able to carry out orders with a cool head."

"Yes sir," the young fox said, stepping off smartly to hand off the letter.

CHAPTER SEVEN
Scientist, Professor, Underworld Figure

Kerro's eyes went wide as they took in the object Elor had just dropped on his desk with a loud clatter. "It's done," the panther said, a cold, stoic look on his features hiding the abject horror at having just unwillingly fulfilled an underworld contract killing, but his eyes at the same time motioning toward the badge that lay on the desk as if to avert Kerro's gaze.

A smile suddenly spread on the stoat's features. "Incredible. That's the quickest I've ever had a job done."

At that he practically leapt to his feat and grabbed Elor's hand, shaking it firmly. "You're well and truly made, as they say in my business," he said. "My organization could use someone like you, someone who gets things done and does it right. And a stone cold killer too, I see! Not a tear for the bastard, that's how we like 'em! You can have it all, my friend!"

Elor was horrified, but tried not to show it. "Actually... I would rather not... I just want a job in the bar, honest work, waiting tables and the like," he replied.

The stoat didn't like what he was hearing, but kept an even tone, sitting down and folding his hands on the desk before him.

"I beg you to reconsider," said Kerro in a calm, confident tone. "Remember, I own most of the enterprises down here, I'm the one you'd have to go through to get a job, I say who works where. I say you're too good to be wasted on waiting tables, and you know what they call my word down here?"

The panther said nothing, shaking his head nervously. The stoat leaned forward over the desk and gave him a sly, confident grin, baring his sharp needle-like teeth with predatory zeal. "Law."

There was an awkward pause. Kerro liked to keep his charges in check, but he also hated to use intimidation where none was needed; Elor was clearly frightened out of his wits already.

He cleared his throat and continued. "I can even get you and that wolf of yours Lycocian passports, real ones, not those cheap fakes the Cylinderheads sell... those will always get you caught. I've got connections all over Lycocia, just work with me for a while, you can get out of this shithole and live the good life in Lycocia, a penthouse in Pyrite City, a summer home on Lake Kojinoka, a bungalow on Loblolly Beach, a limousine, anything you want, and you can kiss the old country goodbye and you don't have to worry about being extradited; as far as they'll know you'll have never even been to the GWI."

It wasn't as if Elor had a choice. Without changing his expression, he simply nodded. "I accept," he said in a calm, metered tone of practiced professionalism, though all his being was screaming against this arrangement.

"I thought so," the stoat said. With that he reached under his desk and pulled out a wad of banknotes that was almost too thick to grasp, a discreet black case, and a plain brown bag.

Elor opened the case first. It was wood wrapped in leather, with polished brass fittings like the sort that musicians used for their instruments. Inside, resting in the case's soft red velvet lining, was a Gyram GK12 nearly identical to the one the Cylinderheads had tried to sell him, except obviously never issued or used and in pristine order.

"You're gonna need it, kid," the stoat said flatly. "You still have that contact I gave you to buy one?" Elor nodded. "Good, I strongly recommend you take this one to him. Tell him to give you 'the works,' he'll add a few custom touches for you. Trust me, you're gonna want it."

Elor nodded and peered inside the bag. There sat the distinct wax-sealed, green glass faceted bottle that he knew all too well. Pulling it out confirmed what he'd thought: Tavel Regal Brandy, though he noticed it wasn't the vintage he had specified.

"Vintage '96?" he shouted. Vintage '98 was valuable enough, and '96 was an even better year by many counts.

"You're welcome," the stoat said, beaming.

For a bloodthirsty thug, he certainly knows good spirits, thought Elor.

"So when do I..." he began.

"...Start? I don't have anything for you at the moment, but I'll be sure to let you know. That stack should be enough to get you through, and there's another one if you do the next job right. It's a dream job, work three or four times a year, make a wad, you're set!"

Elor thought about asking why the Nightwatch agent wanted Alrie, but thought better of it; bringing attention to Alrie's presence might lead to more trouble than it was worth. He already knew more than he cared to know about how things worked in this underworld society.

Meanwhile, he was curious about what getting "The Works" on a Gyram GK-12 meant.

* * *

Elor wasted no time looking for this mystery gunsmith. All he had was a name and a vague idea of where he was located, scrawled on a piece of scratch paper in Kerro's rather rushed handwriting:

Fil Barron
Old Insulated Container
behind Yahel's sausage stand
Just a short walk from The Vixen
Important: TRY NOT TO STARE!

The panther was now just about a block from the sausage stand, wondering about this last comment. He had studied biology and medicine, and had even helped identify the charred remains of victims of the Dai-Yel explosion. What horrific injury or deformity could possibly make him inclined to stare?

He arrived at the insulated container, the sort normally placed in railway box cars to carry fish or produce. A fence had been built around the front, and within the fence a clothesline had been strung between the container and an upturned truck axle. It was bare, though, except for a few clothespins.

Elor let himself in the gate and walked up to the front door, unsure of what awaited him inside the thick walls of the former railway container, or what was so horrific about this Fil fellow that would possibly cause someone to stare. He tapped gingerly on the door, just enough that he was satisfied that anyone inside would have heard him, and waited.

At first there was no answer, for perhaps a full minute that dragged on rather slowly. Elor was about to knock again, wondering if that would even be wise. Just as he had raised his fist to knock louder, the door opened ever so slightly, the inside of the shack dark even compared to the low lights of the hold.

"What do you want?" a voice said.

Elor swallowed. "Kerro sent me," he replied.

The door opened wider. "Come in," the voice said, and Elor stepped inside timidly.

As his eyes adjusted to the dim light, Elor could see a bed, a lamp, and a table laden with tools as the only signs of habitation; everywhere else there were guns of every shape and size, which made the panther nervous.

He never did like weapons and hated the fact that one creature would want to use one against another... why was he suddenly plunged into a kill-or-be-killed world where weapons were an everyday item?

It was then that the final detail hit home, the one Kerro had warned him about. There stood a lanky form in a white shirt and brown trousers. His skin was hairless, he had no muzzle, no tail, a short, flat nose, and a few tufts of gray hair on his head. He looked at Elor with slightly wrinkled gray eyes.

"Yes, I know what you're thinking. Should be extinct by now. You don't have long to wait, cat, I'm all there is," he said. "My village was wiped out twenty-five years ago, the last colony of humans known on earth, murdered for some officers' sick game. I set about going after those officers over the years, managed to wipe out three or four and their families, but I never could finish. Salaar put a price on my head, and the Nightwatch was closing in. I came here to find some refuge, but I know it's only a matter of time. I'm too old and too tired to run. If old age doesn't get me, the Nightwatch will."

"I'm sorry to hear that," Elor replied. "I... used to be a professor of biology. I am honored to meet you."

The man grimaced. "Honored to meet a relic? A thing of the past? A creature not fit for this world? Bah, I've no time for flatterers, are you going to buy something or am I going to have to show you the way out?"

Elor set the case on the table and opened it. "Kerro recommended I get the works," the panther replied, setting the case on the table and opening it to try and ease the conversation into comfortable territory for the old man.

"Ah... No one's requested that in a while," Fil said, not qualifying his remark and looking over the machine gun with an appreciative eye.

"Just what is 'The Works' anyhow?" asked Elor. "Kerro wasn't really clear about it."

"All serial numbers seamlessly removed. A billet receiver to replace the steel one, that will cool faster and let you go longer without a jam. A quick-load modification to the magazine, these stock Gyram mags are a bit clumsy to swap in a fire fight. A nice polished finish, and some custom inlays with your monogram or name on the stock, if you like. What's your name?"

"Elor Kaya," the panther said.

"Oh... *that* Elor," Fil said, the panther trying not to let his ears flatten at hearing the remark a third time.

"I can do this in about a day, that will be five hundred crowns. Quite a bit more than a new GK-12 costs but I give you my word, it's worth every Imperial."

Elor counted out ten 50 crown notes from the stack he had been given, the two exchanged nods, and the deal was done.

Elor walked back into the relative light of the hold,

shuddering somewhat. He had to get his mind off this whole business of guns, gangsters, and contract killings, and he hadn't had breakfast that morning.

There was that sausage stand around the corner, though; one he hadn't tried yet, though it smelled promising. A fried sausage and a cold beer might be just the thing to settle his nerves and get his mind off this whole sordid business.

CHAPTER EIGHT
Worried Emperors, Pleasured Panthers

Jaigon Klanar, chief executive of Dai-Yel Petrochemical and cousin of Emperor Salaar, paced the floor in the emperor's richly-appointed office in his palace outside Highridge. The heels of his shoes clicked restlessly on the marble floor, sometimes dampened by a strip of soft carpet leading straight to the emperor's desk.

Behind the desk itself, high windows reached fully 7 meters before pointing into a graceful arch, affording a magnificent view of the old city sloping up the hill toward Carrick Hall in the distance. On either side, banners of blue with the green Hannari Oak flanked and framed the emperor to magnificent effect.

Word had been sent to Jaigon that a Nightwatch agent had failed to catch Alrie Wenna... this was not good news. The young ferret had been nobody until about eight months before, when she escaped from the factory workers' housing unit outside the Dai-Yel film and pigment plant in Northarbour, a small satellite of the main chemical plant in Lutrum.

She was an odd girl, a troublemaker, a little too smart for her own good, and she had figured out many things the company would rather she didn't know; it seemed she had handily figured out the secret of nearly every machine in the factory and every product they produced there. But when she began figuring out the secrets of products that weren't even made at Northarbour, her overseers had begun to take notice. One product in particular worried Jaigon more than any other, and he was at a loss as to how she could have figured it out.

Now she was gone, and with her a body of knowledge that could easily bring down not only his company, but destroy the Great Wolven Imperium's best leverage to keep nations like Lycocia friendly. While she cowered in the bowels of the Basecraft Cirrostratus living with various outcasts who had no interest in what she knew, she was a controlled threat; if the Lycocian government discovered what she knew, she would become the most unmitigated threat to the empire and all its ambitions.

Jaigon wouldn't be satisfied just to have her killed and be done with it, though; he had to know how this simple-minded factory girl had figured out his company's most complex secrets first, even if it meant personally interrogating her.

"I can't see how a trained Nightwatch agent would fail to catch one unarmed fifteen-year-old ferret. This has become ridiculous," Jaigon fumed. "Do you know where they last saw Agent Hollax? He was out drinking with a couple of perverts! Stumbling around the holds, trolling for some sick fun with another male, they say."

Salaar thumbed through his copy of the dossier. "Not unusual for an agent who volunteers for work on the Basecraft to be a loose end. Agent Hollax was a volunteer, I suspect he was a pervert looking for a free pass. No matter, if he is ever seen again I'll see to it his execution is done in the old Lutran tradition, bound to a stake, sword through his heart, in the most public place possible and broadcast on every television and every newsreel across my domain."

"Pity about Hollax, but what about Alrie?" Jaigon insisted.

"She is no more harmful than any other fugitive!" Salaar replied. "How many of our architects and engineers have taken their secrets to the basecraft? We've been having a devil of a time keeping anyone of importance in check and we both know it. She's just a factory girl, odds are no one would believe her if she told them what she knew."

"That's just the trouble, she *is* just a factory girl," Jaigon growled. "She escaped from factory housing. We keep those factory workers under lock and key at all hours, if she escaped, there might be others. Besides which, what if she tells what she knows and someone believes her? We can't sit idly by. There's too much at stake."

The emperor pushed a pair of spectacles further up his muzzle. "Mark my words, I will deal with Alrie and all the miscreants on the Cirrostratus. But in my own time, Jaigon. We can't just go blasting an airship that cost more than a billion crowns to build out of the sky, we pull at least half a million crowns a month in revenue from sales tax there alone. But sooner or later, I will find a way to have them all arrested and executed."

"Don't you see? That girl is too valuable, we might learn about some security leak from her, supposing she's not the source of the leak? We might have a dozen pairs of loose lips to seal!" Jaigon shouted, getting the sinking feeling that Salaar didn't care about his interests in the least.

"This isn't just about you, Jaigon, you're not the only one with loose ends on that ship, and even if you are my cousin I can't stop everything to retrieve one miscreant for your vanity. She'll be nobody's problem sooner or later. If there's an intelligence leak in your labs that would be your responsibility, not mine."

With that, Jaigon nodded. "Very well, Salaar. As you wish." With that, he gave a curt bow and strode toward the door. "I knew you'd see things my way, you always were the sensible one," Salaar said with a cordial smile, his tone leaving Jaigon unsure if he was joking or serious.

I'm bringing that girl in. If the Nightwatch won't do it, I'll find my own way, Jaigon thought.

* * *

Elor had gotten more than he'd bargained for at the sausage stand. No sooner had he gotten his sausage and a bottle of lukewarm, second-rate Lycocian beer when he felt a hand on his shoulder. The Panther jumped, nearly dropping his food.

"So, Vinz tells me there's this thing you used to do..."

Elor jumped again, then turned to see the young fox who had been with the wolf the night before... for all that had happened it seemed an entire week had passed.

"Pardon?" was all the panther could choke out, tail swaying anxiously.

"How rude of me! I'm Laz. A friend of Vinz's. I think we've met, haven't we?" The fox gave him a warm smile, his tail wagging with excitement as he stepped closer to the panther.

"We have," Elor said, stepping back.

"Good... So... Want to head up to my place? We should get more acquainted," Laz said.

"Fuck's sake! We just met!" the panther said, turning to storm off... then as he'd gotten a few paces away he slowed down and turned again.

The fox looked young, perhaps his early 20s, though more likely, by the way he carried himself, he was closer to Vinz's age. He wore a tight, sleeveless cotton undershirt, close-fitting brown wool trousers, and a pair of black boots kept neatly polished. He looked to have been a soldier of some sort at one time, but the panther couldn't place the clothing as part of any uniform he'd ever seen. By his accent, he was probably from inland, around New Lycopolis or thereabouts. He was handsome, and seemed harmless enough... If nothing else, spending a little time with him was a good way to keep out of trouble.

He turned to gaze back at Laz. The fox looked positively heartbroken at Elor's rejection, his ears sagging to the sides and his tail drooping as he gazed at the ground, shuffling restlessly back and forth.

It always tugged at Elor's heart to see a canid of any sort look dejected, and they were just so good at doing it. *Have I really hurt him that much by walking away, or is this just some old fox trick for getting a fellow into bed?* Elor thought.

There wasn't much to lose by changing his mind; Elor began turning back. He stepped up to Laz, put a friendly hand on his shoulder, and smiled.

"On second thought, I think I'd like that," the panther said. It had been a rough day, and he found the invitation to release his frustrations far too inviting.

Laz beamed, his tail and ears once again perking visibly. "I won't disappoint!" he said, leading Elor across the holds.

Moments later, after the panther had spent some moments struggling to keep up with the lithe fox's jaunt through the back alleys between the shoddily-built shacks that littered the hold, he found himself in a small but comfortably furnished box in the far corner from The Vixen.

It had been previously used as a crate full of some manner of spares for a Star-Lutra dealership in one of the many export markets where the cars were sold. Barely tall enough to stand in and barely long enough to lay in, it stood atop a mountain of other such crates in the port and stern, overlooking the better part of the shanty town.

Laz drew a curtain made from old upholstery fabric and turned on a hastily-wired light bulb, then pulled off his shirt. A streak of light, well-kept cream-colored fur could be seen. Elor stared admiringly as he laid back on what was apparently the bed.

"Here, those Lycocian beers are no good, have one of these," said Laz. He offered the panther a plain, green, unlabeled bottle and a bottle opener.

The panther pried it open and took a whiff of the concoction. "Amazing," he said.

"From the Cylinderheads' own brewery, they know good spirits," the fox said, cracking open a bottle of his own and downing it with alarming speed that surprised the panther.

"Now, why don't you make yourself a little more comfortable, hmm?" Laz said, leaning over Elor and teasingly unbuttoning his jacket and shirt, rubbing playfully at the panther's chest.

Elor began to breathe hard, whiskers trembling and muzzle wide. He sat up and took the shirt and jacket off, revealing a slightly aged but still well-toned chest and midriff.

Laz just smiled and leaned in, closing his eyes giving the panther a deep, muzzle-to-muzzle kiss. Elor's eyes went wide and his pulse went wild, not sure if he wanted to do this but finding himself wrapping his arms around Laz's slender body.

Within moments, before either was really sure what was happening, both had discarded their clothes entirely and were kissing and caressing, lost in the moment, their arousal growing stronger and stronger.

Then Elor spoke up. "So... are you usually... you know..." He made a small circle with his left thumb and forefinger, motioning with his right thumb and forefinger.

Laz was inwardly annoyed, but kept a smile. "Not all foxes are passive, Elor," he said. Taking a small amount of some substance kept in a bottle on a small crate that served as a nightstand, he rubbed it along the length of his partly-exposed shaft, then pushed Elor down onto the soft cushion that served as a bed. He moved forward between Elor's legs, a lusty fire in his catlike eyes. "Some of us wear the dark blue feather too."

The fox pushed forward, causing the panther to grimace. It had been a very, very long time and he was barely ready... and yet he wanted this.

Laz exhaled softly and settled for a moment, savoring the sensation as he looked down at Elor.

In short order, the two moved with each other, becoming accustomed to one another's bodies, moving in time, their breath coming in gasps and moans as the heat of climax built between them, then both let out a sharp yelp as Laz became stuck inside the panther, both creatures climaxing in the same heart-stopping instant.

Elor was sore, but his mind was a blissful fog of sensations. "I... I forgot that foxes did that too," he said, embarrassed that a professor of biology would forget such a thing. He let out a grunt and somewhat unintentionally clenched around the vulpine member still deep within him.

Laz let out a long, pleasured moan, wagging his tail and giving a series of sharp, semi-voluntary thrusts. "again," the fox said.

It took the panther a moment to realize what the fox wanted, then obliged him with another clench, eliciting much the same reaction from the fox as before.

"Again!" the fox said, louder.

Elor clenched yet again, this time holding it for a sustained period of time. By this time, Laz was practically speaking gibberish as he thrusted the last inch or so behind his knot wildly in and out before falling forward, breathing hard and nuzzling Elor warmly.

At last, Laz was spent, and the two lay together for some time, half-asleep.

As the last waves of the afterglow began to fade and Elor felt Laz slowly slide out of him, the two began to caress and kiss once again, the beer now having taken full effect of Laz while Elor, who had barely touched his, remained more or less lucid.

"Now, have you ever been with felines?" Elor asked.

The fox thought about it for a moment. "A lion, once," he said, nodding.

"Oh... Well, lions are a bit unusual, they don't have it... but most of us felines have a little something that some species find a bit... exotic. Oh, I grant you, Vinz loved it, but it's not for everyone."

With that, Elor sat up and displayed his member for the fox. It was thinner, with a pointier tip, and lined with small studs along its length. "Think you can take it?" the panther smiled.

The fox said nothing, but pushed the panther rather roughly back onto the bed, resting his hands on his shoulders, then lowered himself onto Elor's shaft with a soft, willing moan. He began to move up and down rhythmically, his tight entrance welcoming Elor's bristled length with an eagerness that astounded the panther.

Finally, Laz reached a position where Elor's tip was jabbing squarely at his prostate and he began to ride quickly. Elor leaned back, letting out a pleasured snarl as he savored the sensation for a moment.

Then, just as Laz began to slow, Elor suddenly sat up and tipped the fox onto his back, not changing the angle even the slightest, and began thrusting into the vulpine's wanting body.

The act didn't last long; Elor's years of chastity finally told on him in his stamina. He could hold nothing back as he released a sustained, satisfying climax into the handsome fox that lay under him. He pinned his ears back, body going rigid and hilted into Laz, then relaxed with a soft moan.

The two creatures sat up, smiling. Laz reached for a towel he kept nearby and wiped himself clean, then handed it to Elor.

"How was it?" Laz said, grinning at the panther.

"I haven't done this in nearly a decade... maybe we should meet more often," Elor said.

With that, the panther quickly dressed himself, they said their goodbyes, Elor checked all his belongings to make sure the fox wasn't after his money, then they parted ways.

Laz sighed softly, stretching his still-naked form across his bed roll, resting his chin on his hands and dreamily smiling as he finished off the rest of Elor's beer, falling blissfully asleep in the afterglow of their encounter.

CHAPTER NINE
Crash Reports, Betrayals, and Dumb Luck

Imperial Air Force of his Imperial Highness Salaar the Great

Incident Report
<u>CONFIDENTIAL</u>

Filed:
11 Lai, 1704

Date of Incident:
9 Lai 1704

Nature of Incident:
Air Crash, otherwise Specified (section 84-73)

Craft:
Star Javelin Single-Seat interceptor/light bomber

Serial of Craft:
909-GG3

Number of Crew:
One (1)

Name(s), species, and status of Crew:
IG49453 Lieut. Bram Malga- otter- DECEASED

Description of Incident:

On the afternoon of 9 Lai, Lt. Bram Malga, in blatant disregard to orders from his wing commander, veered out of formation with his light bomber detachment and flew in the general direction of the Isle of Rest. Somewhere approximately one degree south southwest of the Isle of Rest, his plane was spotted by the control towers of Basecraft Cirrostratus and was assumed to be attempting a landing. Attempts at radio contact were met with radio silence. At approximately 22:00 hours Lt. Malga's aircraft nosed sharply upward and was seen to take an elliptical loop over the basecraft, the fuselage of the plane missing the basecraft by approximately 16 meters upon descending.

Preliminary reports suggest that Lt. Malga attempted to parachute to safety. The discovery of a discarded parachute canopy and survival raft some kilometers from the site of impact confirm this. However, near the site of impact, Malga's body was discovered floating in the debris field. The body itself had by all appearances struck the water at high velocity. His skull was nearly obliterated, limbs disarticulated, and clothing ripped clear of the body (see attached mortuary report for full details on the condition of the body as recovered and a complete analysis of perimortem and postmortem trauma as determined by the coroner's office of the Department of Military Surgeons' field office in Northarbour).

As of the date of this report no clothing has been recovered, nor have any identifying documents that would prove conclusively the identity of the body recovered, but it is the Air Force's belief that it is satisfactorily certain that the body is in fact that of Lt. Malga. It is the high command's opinion that the discovery of a male otter's body within the debris field of Lt. Malga's craft outside a combat zone constitutes a circumstance well beyond the realm of coincidence.

The wreckage of the plane thus far recovered displays damage consistent with a nose-first impact with the water; that is, much of the debris recovered is small, superficial pieces of the craft whereas it is known from our surveys and preliminary reports from Navy divers that the bulk of the craft is located under approximately 200 meters of water just a few kilometers from the edge of the continental shelf. This consists primarily of the fuselage, canopy, and tail as most of the material composing the engine bay up to the forward bulkhead, the wings beyond the inboard support struts, and the rear elevator has been obliterated by the impact.

It is therefore the belief of the Air Force, pending a final investigation, that Lieutenant Malga had originally intended to land on the Basecraft Cirrostratus following his desertion, but had cut radio so as not to be identified and therefore was incapable of transmission to the basecraft's air control tower. Having missed his landing and nearly crashing into the craft, he pulled up sharply, causing his interceptor to stall and nose forward, at which point he left the craft. He then became disoriented and confused after his bailout by the poor lighting conditions, misjudged his altitude above the darkened ocean, and cut his chute at an altitude of around 1 kilometer, falling to his death in the water below.

It is the opinion of the high command and the Department of Military Surgeons that there is nothing further to be learned from Lieut. Malga's remains and they have been discharged from the examining facilities and placed in an on-site mortuary storage facility.

Owing to the dishonorable circumstances of Lieut. Malga's demise, there are currently no plans to inter his body in a state cemetery, but rather it will be handed over to next of kin to be disposed of at their expense, or else disposed of by incineration at the convenience of his commanding officer.

Presently the Air Force and Navy are jointly discussing options for the recovery of the Star-Javelin interceptor involved in this incident for examination and investigation; however, it is expected that the examination of the wreckage will confirm the findings of this investigation.

* * *

The weary marten pulled the carriage of his typewriter back to its tab stop, then removed the last sheet of the report. It had been the eighth such report he had transcribed in as many days; it seemed these deserters were getting more and more desperate by the day.

He slid the onion-skin thin slip of messily-typed paper into a plain envelope, along with the mortuary report and a few grisly, grainy, high-contrast photos related to the incident, then strode across a room full of desks nearly identical to his, filing similarly grim reports of dead or missing soldiers, to a row of tubes on the far wall. He took a small metal and plastic capsule and opened it, rolling the folder to fit inside, then placed it under the tube and sent it on its way.

The capsule lurched upward with a squeak, on its way to somewhere else even deeper in the bowels of the high command complex in New Lycopolis, and the marten made his way back to his desk, straightening his tie and taking a seat to transcribe the next thing in the forever-full wire basket of papers to be processed, as the typefalls of more than a hundred identical typewriters filled the air around him in the sparse room.

The life of a bureaucrat wasn't the least bit rewarding at all... though at least it was steady work.

* * *

"I smell fox on you, Elor."

The wolf stood in the doorway of the ramshackle flat with his arms folded and a look of distrust on his features. He glared at the panther with a suspicious eye, a look he should have expected by now after all that had happened between them, but it unnerved him deeply.

"What are you implying, Vinz?" said Elor, well aware that it was no use denying the strong scent of vulpine pheromones that clung to him. Inwardly he cringed, thinking he may as well be parading around with a big red sign telling everyone his latest exploits with Laz.

Vinz's hands clenched into fists. "I invite you into my home after nine years of never so much as attempting to contact or visit me. I stay here with you even though I probably should have fled to the Altocirrus or the Cumulonimbus the moment you accepted Kerro's offer. You killed a bleeding Nightwatch agent in my home and made us both targets. And now... Now you go about stealing my lovers too? It just wasn't enough to ruin my life once this week, was it?"

Elor folded his ears back. He could tell that behind Vinz's furious tone there was a note of exasperation, desperation even. As always, Vinz was silently asking him "am I right?" and begging to be validated.

Elor, however, was in no mood to validate Vinz's line of thinking; he was going to make it hurt.

"Ruin your life?" he said, his tone strong as he straightened his back and squared his shoulders. "For your information if I hadn't been here you and Alrie both would probably be dead! Do you really think that agent was going to let you off easy for harboring that girl, whatever she did? You'd have both been dragged out behind the nearest police station and shot as soon as it was convenient. If you call saving two lives ruining one, I'm clearly not your biggest problem, Vinz!"

The wolf pinned back his ears, averting his eyes to a corner of the room. He had forgotten just how well Elor knew his every weakness. In a battle of words, the panther knew how to hit where it hurt; Bringing up the subject of Alrie was decidedly below the belt.

"Don't you dare change the subject on me!" Vinz growled, his teeth bared. "This is about what you did with Laz! I don't care how long you'd been celibate, you had no right to touch him!"

The panther had heard enough. Vinz was definitely weakened but hadn't been disarmed yet. It was time to strike at the very heart of the wolf's insecurity and move in for the kill.

"I had *every* right to touch him, Vinz, and you know why?"

said Elor, moving toward the wolf with a predatory glare.

Before Vinz could answer, he continued. "I had every right because he asked me to. His body isn't yours, and if you keep treating him like a possession you'll be the one who has no right!"

The wolf held his ground and glared at him, fighting back tears, unable to think of a response. His defenses had been shattered and he was left with nothing, vulnerable and afraid.

"And anyway, you're the one who told me about that thing he used to do. You put the idea in my head."

The two turned and looked in surprise. There was Laz, looking hurt and perhaps a bit angry. "Wolfy, I'm sorry..." he began.

Elor stepped back and had a seat, opening his bottle of vintage Tavellian brandy with a pocket corkscrew and taking a generous swig as if swilling cheap cider. This was no longer his moment and he wanted no part of it.

Vinz shook his head. "You betrayed me," he said in a low growl, not even looking at the fox.

"Did I ever agree to be your property, Vinz?" Laz said.

"I'm at the age where I want a constant companion," said Vinz, his voice softer and sadder than before, wringing his hands and avoiding eye contact with Laz. "I'm too old for loose boys who sleep with anything that moves. I want loyalty. I told you that already."

"Well, I don't sleep with anything that moves. I never agreed to be yours entirely, but you've been the only one I've seen since our first night. And I thought... I thought if the two of you used to be lovers, that maybe he was as wonderful as you." The fox finished his sentence softly, his voice heavy with the sadness of a child who had done wrong without intending to.

Vinz lifted his head a moment, his eyes making contact with Laz's for the first time. "Was he?" he asked.

Laz nodded. "Every bit," he said softly.

Vinz growled, turning away from the fox. "Then I am replaceable to you. Go, have any male you want on this ship, but don't stop yourself over someone who's just as good as anyone else," he said, fighting back a sob.

The fox looked indignant. "You're being unreasonable," he said.

"Then what do you propose, O Sly One?" said Vinz, this time deeply irritated and showing it.

"I..." the fox stopped, swallowing hard, his tail curling between his legs as he considered the weight of what he was about to ask of Vinz. "...I want you both."

Something warm and wet spattered both of them. A strong scent of alcohol and fermented fruit filled the air and the two looked at Elor, who had just wasted about ten crowns worth of brandy in his reaction to Laz's proposal.

The panther coughed. "Sorry," he said hoarsely, as he tried in vain to wipe himself and the floor in front of him with a small handkerchief.

"Now who's being unreasonable?" Vinz said, throwing his hands up in the air.

"How is that in any way unreasonable, Vinz?" said Laz. "I love you, and I love Elor too... what is so hard to understand here?"

Vinz paused. "I don't know what to say," he replied quietly.

"Then don't say anything," said Laz. "Just think about it. You may not love him any more, he may not love you any more, but you're both fine, attractive creatures for your age, you're intelligent, and you're both much classier than most of the lot I find round the Vixen. It's not like the two of you would ever have to be in the same room together, even. I don't see why I couldn't have you both."

"It's just so..." Vinz began.

"...odd." Elor finished.

"Will you at least think about it? Both of you? Please?" the fox said, giving them a look of disarming vulnerability that neither was prepared for.

"I have a long night ahead of me, Laz. Please.... I can't be bothered to... that is..." Vinz struggled to say it, but try as he might he couldn't say no.

"Just think about it," said Laz. "There's no hurry, love, I

know it's a lot to ask but it I really do want you and Elor both."

Vinz drew a heavy sigh. "Fine, I'll think about it," the wolf said, exasperated.

"Now where was I? Oh, Elor, Kerro wants you," Laz continued. "That's why I came here in the first place."

"Kerro? What does he want?" Elor said, swallowing one more swig of brandy as if bracing for some unspeakable news before trying to squeeze the cork back into the bottle.

"He didn't say. It was important, though, he wants to discuss it in his office" Laz replied.

Elor nodded, getting up, grabbing his coat and heading for the doorway.

"Don't bother coming back," said Vinz.

"Well, then, I guess he's staying at my place tonight," said Laz with a defiant grin.

"Fine, come back, but don't get comfortable, you miserable cheat!" the wolf called after the panther as he made his way down the corridor.

Elor made his way to the Vixen, walking through the main bar. A few Cylinderheads sat there; rather than eye him with hostility or amusement this time, however, they seemed to all give Elor a respectful nod as the panther made his way to Kerro's private door at the back of the bar.

The walk to Kerro's office seemed shorter than Elor remembered. Maybe it was the fact that he'd been there before, or the fact that it was no longer an imposing and unknown place for him, but it seemed he arrived at the door of the lavishly appointed engine crate much quicker this time.

A couple of knocks and Kerro opened the door, greeting him warmly.

"Welcome! Do come in, have a seat!" the stoat gestured toward the plush chairs in front of his desk.

Elor sat down. Kerro grabbed a box of cigars near the door and offered one to Elor, who took one, biting off the end and holding it up to the lighter the stoat proffered. Kerro then took his seat, sniffing one of the cigars almost lustily before biting off the end and lighting it.

"So Elor, I've got a very important job for you," Kerro said. "You're kind of new to our little organization so I'll tell you a little about how we operate. We have a sort of... code of ethics if you will. If you're going to compete, do it honestly, and no one will bother you, may the best creature win. When the competition decides to play dirty, though... well, we don't like it. And in our organization I think you know what we do when we don't like something. We fix it. Now tell me, if you own a... shall we say, reasonably legitimate club as I do, and someone else decides they're going to open up a competing club in another basecraft, they've got a right, don't they?"

At that Elor nodded. "I suppose so," he said.

"Of course they do. We all buy from the same suppliers. It's the Cylinderheads that make these clubs great. We get our shipments of bootleg whiskey and the odd bale of ghella leaves to sell here or there. They recruit escorts too. Sex, smokes, and booze, that's most of what the surface dwellers come here for, so someone else opening a club doesn't mean a thing. They get it all the same place we do."

Elor nodded, not sure where Kerro was going with this.

"Now tell me," Kerro continued, "if the owner of this... other club suddenly started telling his customers that your club was rotten, that there was bad booze in the bar and all your escorts had lice, and generally saying things about your business that just weren't true, they wouldn't have a right, would they?"

Elor shook his head. "I suppose not," he muttered

"Damn straight they wouldn't!" Kerro shouted. "They don't have a right 'cause they were lucky we tolerated them stealing our business with their rotten copycat club to begin with!" the stoat fumed, clawing at his desk. With that he reached into his desk and pulled out a small, sleek automatic pistol, handing it to Elor.

"Another little present. The GK 12 is great for doing some damage, but you can't get in too close with that one. This one's great for getting in close. Slips right into your vest pocket, then back out of sight as soon as you're done. You're going to need it because I want you to get this double-crosser here." Kerro pulled out a grainy photograph of a raccoon in a pinstripe suit. He appeared to be fairly short, if the height of the bar in the background was any indication.

"Hannock Burad, owner of the Frisky Wolf. He's going to be passing through the basecraft tomorrow night on his way back from New Therion to Highridge, staying in the usual place on the hotel deck, Suite 214. You'll have to get creative with this job. I don't think he's going to be down in the sublevels much, let alone in my club. Besides, the Cylinderheads wouldn't want him getting whacked down here, it's bad for business. Your best bet would be to get him while he's still in his suite. Here, you might need this, too."

With that, Kerro took a suit that was hanging from a corner of a file cabinet, covered in white drycleaner's paper. "An exact match for a bellhop's uniform. Our friend Hannock will be more likely to... shall we say... let you do your job if he thinks you're with the hotel staff."

Elor nodded nervously. "Thank you, sir," he said.

"Finish this job and I'll make you rich, kid," said Kerro. "You'll have earned quite a few favors once you do this. Though you'd better keep your end of the deal, you hear me? No cold feet now means no regrets later."

Elor nodded once again, swallowing hard as he looked at the small black pistol and slipped it into the inside pocket of his vest.

"Well, what are you waiting for?" Kerro said, slapping him on the back and urging him toward the door. "That jerk's not gonna kill himself."

* * *

As luck would have it, Elor's job was not that difficult. The next evening, after a long trudge from the sublevels up to the suite deck in the ship's tower, Elor found the door of Suite 214 ajar.

Something was amiss, and the panther's senses were taut as he looked, listened, and smelled the corridors, looking for some sign of danger. He drew the small automatic pistol and slowly nudged the door open with his elbow.

There was Hannock, lying on the floor of the suite in a pool of blood.

Someone must have gotten here before me, Elor thought with cold factuality. It was then he noticed the ornate derringer just next to Hannock's hand.

Elor slid his own pistol back into his trouser pocket, then removed the vest, cap, and bowtie of the hotel uniform. There was a laundry chute about midway down the hall, he would drop them there.

He looked around for some hint as to why Hannock had taken his own life, a note, a scrap of a clue that would tell him, but he didn't browse for long. This was not a scene he needed to be connected with.

He picked up the derringer and wrapped it in a handkerchief, then hurried out of the room, opening the door of the chute just long enough to get rid of the uniform, then made his way to the flight deck.

There, he walked to the edge of the deck and hurled the derringer away, sending it tumbling into the ocean below, out of sight and out of mind. The job, as far as Kerro would be concerned, was done, and Hannock's death would remain shrouded in mystery.

* * *

To Kerro, of course, it looked like the most professional job he'd ever seen. He had found out only hours later, when Hannock's lifeless body was found by a horrified maid.

The next day, he called Elor into his office to personally congratulate him.

"In all my days working this business, not once have I seen someone perform a hit so cleanly!" Kerro purred as he leaned excitedly forward over his desk. "Almost looked like a suicide though, the cops are still trying to figure it out and even Hannock's cronies have their doubts. Well, never mind, I didn't exactly tell you how I wanted it done, did I? The point is, he's dead, and that's one less lying, slandering sack of shit to worry about."

Kerro reached into his desk and pulled out a cigar box. "I think this calls for a little something special." He opened it wide and slid it across the wide desktop to Elor. The panther's eyes went wide. There wasn't a single cigar in the box, but quite a lot of 500 Crown notes... more than Elor had ever seen in one place.

Kerro grinned. "Fifty-thousand, that's my final offer, take it or leave it," he said jokingly.

"Thank you, sir," said Elor, not quite sure what to think but tucking the cigar box under his arm with an astonished look on his face.

Kerro leaned back in his chair and folded his arms behind his head. "No sir! Thank you! You saved my club and showed everyone what happens when you play dirty in this business. Anyways, you're gonna need this. A high-profile job like this one only comes around every couple years or so, I pay generously because I know it'll be a while yet before you get another one this big. You're new in the business, but you'll find there's a lot more cloak than dagger around here. Though there's a lot of shakedowns, you know, roughing 'em up a bit to show you mean business but let 'em go with most of their bones still intact. We might need you for a bit of that too, but we'll see."

Elor nodded, not sure what to say.

"Now, there's one more thing I want you to know," Kerro continued, getting up from his desk and walking over to Elor. "We don't like guys who flash their money around. We don't like guys who go out of their way to hobnob, blow it on good wine and high-class girls. If you work in this business, you have to keep a low profile and you have to live according to your cover. If I see you swinging a couple of actresses on your arm and eating up on the scenic deck with the captain and Ovego knows who else, I'm gonna have to take you down, you hear me?"

Elor stood up slowly, nodding emphatically. "Of course," he said, not wanting to raise Kerro's ire.

"That doesn't mean you can't go enjoy yourself a bit, though. Go on, go buy yourself something nice, a reasonably-priced suit, maybe a hooker or two. You're one of my best guys, Elor, and I'll be calling you soon enough! Now, go relax you big dumb bastard!" Elor said with a mile-wide grin, patting him between the shoulder blades as they walked toward the door.

As the door closed behind him, Elor thought once again to ask about Agent Hollax and Alrie and what exactly was going on, but once again he thought better of it.

The less I know about this, the better, he thought. The panther clenched the cigar box under his arm and made his way back toward Vinz's place, feeling safe for the moment... but by no means satisfied.

CHAPTER TEN
The Surprising Mr. Kaya

There was scarcely a creature in the holds of the Basecraft Cirrostratus who hadn't changed somewhat since their arrival. Life in the holds had a way of changing everyone; sometimes even becoming the complete opposite of what they had been years ago, back on the surface.

No one, for example, knew that Kerro Hemini wasn't a Lycocian at all. He was once a truck driver for a florist in Lutrum, making a pittance driving flowers from the nursery outside the city to the grocer's market in the center of the old town. Yet he maintained a clean enough profile to travel freely to Lycocia whenever he wanted to, and learned to mimic the accents and mannerisms of big city gangsters from his dealings with them. The accent he affected had become good enough to fool even a real Lycocian gangster.

Nor did anyone know that Fil Barron had once been a tinkerer, fixing machines and appliances and making chairs and cabinets for the people of his small village. His truest joy, though, was in making toys for the few children who lived in the village; having no children himself, it delighted him to be a sort of surrogate grandfather. When his village was destroyed, his skill was turned to making caskets; when he sought revenge on those who destroyed the village, he turned his skills to making bombs. Now, old, degraded, and resentful, those same skills went into making and repairing guns.

Most knew that Alrie had been a factory worker, but the how and why of her escape from the seemingly inescapable world of the working underclass was a complete mystery to everyone but herself and Vinz. She lived well enough on the handouts she received from creatures throughout the hold, both strangers and friends alike, and never made a fuss about not having a place to call her own.

And as for Laz and the newly-arrived Bram, no one was entirely sure where they were from or what they did, only that Bram had been a pilot and Laz had been a mechanic of some sort. Neither seemed keen to talk about their lives before they arrived in the basecraft, and it was assumed by most that those personal details were of no consequence any more.

Elor thought about this for a moment as he sat with them in Vinz's flat one night, cigarette in one hand and a glass of whiskey in the other. The three talked casually, going on and on about the most inane things, and that was when it struck the panther how much his life in the basecraft had changed him.

He wasn't the sane, sober, celibate Professor Elor Kaya any more. Professor Kaya had died; he was a memory in the heart of an aging wolf. He was a ghost that haunted the halls of University College Highridge. He was the stated occupant of a small apartment downtown Highridge and the former owner of a green Lutra Special.

Now there was only Elor, the small-talking, sharp-dressed assassin who sat in dark smoky rooms with handsome, mysterious males and loved every moment of it. He was relaxed, cavalier, and more openly sensual than ever in his life. He was *alive*, something Professor Kaya could never have claimed.

A sonigram machine played nearby, the soft hum of the recorder heads moving slowly across the width of the continuously-looped belt of magnetic tape the only thing that could be heard in the few silent moments when no one spoke and the player was between tracks. Silence was the exception; a second or two of mechanical hums was almost invariably replaced by friendly gossip and blaring brass band jazz, as if their conversation and the music were somehow recorded in the same session.

There was something else happening to Elor on this particular evening, though... perhaps it was the whiskey, or perhaps just fatigue, but he felt himself becoming silly. Sounds and sights seemed heightened, in a delirious and intoxicating way. Small, unassuming things seemed to stand out, and the panther was becoming very aware of it... yet his mind and his mouth seemed disconnected somehow, and he noticed that he was still making small talk mindlessly even as the room seemed to come alive with sensations and every atom in his body seemed to vibrate warmly.

He was starting on some tangent about the quality of the street food within the holds when he stopped short and looked at the wet ridges on his fingertip through the magnifying distortion of the glass in his hand.

"Like a bleedin' gecko..." he said.

Laz suddenly burst out laughing, then Elor joined, followed by Bram.

"Gecko... what a funny word," said Laz.

Elor grinned and leaned over next to him. "Geck..." he said, Laz trying not to laugh. "...O".

At that, Laz laughed so hard he spilled his drink and nearly dropped his cigarette, his second that night.

"Come here, you lovely beast," said Elor, grabbing the laughing fox and pulling him into his lap, playfully rubbing his belly and giving his ear an affectionate nip. Laz let him do as he pleased, basking in the panther's attention... all the while still laughing hysterically at the word "gecko."

Had he been in his right mind, Bram might have cleared his throat and asked to be excused following such a display; he was the sort who tolerated this sort of behavior, but only behind closed doors. In his current state, however, the otter could only fall out of his chair laughing at the amorous panther and the hysterical fox.

Vinz came home just a few moments later. The first thing that struck him was the smell, a thick and unpleasant arrangement of odors if there ever was one. He could smell whiskey, which was not unexpected at all. He could also tell the usual suspects were involved because their scent was heavy in it, but one scent was stronger than that of whiskey, fox, otter, or panther.

It was a warm, stale musky stench sort of like burning rope

that the wolf knew all too well from his years working in the Cunning Little Vixen.

He stepped inside and found Laz sitting in Elor's lap, preening him with his front teeth and tongue- still clothed, thankfully- while Bram lay rolling on the floor in a giggling stupor. The wolf frowned, his ears folding back with annoyance.

"When did you take up smoking, Elor?" Vinz said.

"Come on, Vinz, I smoke a cigar time to time, always did, just not so often," Elor replied.

"Well you never smoked ghella leaves!" Vinz said.

Elor looked sleepily at him, the sentence taking a bit longer than usual to sink in. "Ghella leaves? No wonder these ciggies were a bit strong."

At this, Laz giggled softly, then let out a yip as Elor's hand rested none too subtly on the crotch of his trousers.

"That's enough, you rotter!" said Vinz, cuffing Elor on the head. "Fox, otter, the party's over. Get out!"

Laz and Bram gave the wolf a heartbroken look, then slowly made their way back to Laz's place.

* * *

Bram had just recently moved into a crate right next to Laz on the same level of that large stack in the corner of the hold, and the two were generally good neighbors. Bram had once told Laz that if he made a pass, he'd be beaten or worse, and although it was said with a wry smile, Laz didn't want to take a chance with the otter's good will.

In all truth, Bram was pretty ambivalent about the whole idea. He certainly wasn't interested in males himself, though. He wasn't without his prejudices on the subject either; he felt that ideally, male and female were made for each other and that it was peculiar and rather unhealthy that anyone would deviate from that; tradition ran deep in his family and this was one he very much agreed with. Years ago he'd been concerned about how openly these male couples had flaunted their activities, and had long thought some decency laws in Lutrum would be a good idea.

But now, owing his life to two such creatures who had once been lovers, even the last of Bram's prejudices had begun to erode. Weren't they just like anyone else, just trying to be good lawful citizens and mind their own business? Who cared how much or how little anyone knew about their lives? Was it really anyone's business if they liked it or not? And those decency laws he had thought would be such a good idea... what good had they done once Salaar passed them? It was a slippery slope, really. If you could tell someone they couldn't be seen in public, it was only a matter of time before they couldn't survive in private.

Vinz, Laz, and Elor could never be just anonymous deviants any more; they had names and lives, and they were as much a part of his life now as anyone else living in the holds. Vinz never turned him away if he needed something, Elor was a generous host with good taste and always good for a laugh, and Laz was a good neighbor in every sense of the word. Not once had any of them tried to bed him and they were always obliging to his sensibilities.

Laz and Bram spent the rest of the evening at Laz's place, smoking the rest of the ghella leaves and listening to the radio. Bram would wake up the next morning in his own bed, with a headache and only a faint memory of the night before; Laz, meanwhile, would completely forget that Bram was ever there to begin with... until he found the contents of the otter's pockets resting on his night stand. The two agreed to assume nothing interesting had happened between them, and that was that.

* * *

Vinz, meanwhile, was vexed by Elor. What happened to the shy, naïve fellow he'd known most of his life? He'd become a little too brash, caught up in the sordid glamor of an underworld assassin's life. Sooner or later, Vinz realized, Elor would get someone close to him killed, and he hoped desperately that it wouldn't be him. Elor was becoming too arrogant, too sure of himself... exactly the sort of character that ended up getting knifed to death by a Cylinderhead death squad.

"What's become of you, Catts?" he said, shaking his head sadly. "You came here just a shadow of who you were, sad and scared, and now you're running around like a Lycocian crime lord, wearing fancy clothes and drinking high-end brandy, you bought a brand new sonigram machine... and then just this morning I found this hidden away in a corner!"

Vinz produced Elor's GK-12, its ornate stock and magazine temporarily removed. "You hate guns! You said so yourself!" the wolf seemed exasperated.

Elor shook his head. "It's a necessary evil, Vinz, you know that as well as I do."

"And furthermore," Vinz continued, "I know you and Laz are still fucking so don't deny it."

Elor folded back his ears, trying to deflect attention from this last point.

"I didn't choose my line of work, Vinz. Kerro chose it for me. I know the risks, but I'm dead if I do, dead if I don't. And don't hate me if I spend a little money on diversions. I've never had a real life before, I was always such a bore, always had a day-to-day schedule with everything so neatly planned, but I had no risks to consider either. I would have died at a ripe old age. But now... now I could die any day, Vinz. There's no telling how long it'll be, maybe I'll grow old or maybe I'll be dead before morning. If you could die any day, wouldn't you live every day like it was the sweetest day of all time? Tell me you wouldn't!"

Vinz pinned his ears back. "I could die any day myself, thanks to you," he growled. "You've made me a target now. You've taken my security, the quiet of my home, and twice now you have ripped true love from my hands! I'm through with you, and I'm through with Laz and Bram and all your other good-for-nothing underworld friends. Go away! Get out! Maybe your gangster friends can find some other nice place for you to live."

The room fell silent. Elor stood there, slack-jawed, looking as if he could burst into tears any moment but too shocked to shed a single one. After nine years, the reality of how foolishly he'd acted seemed to be setting in.

Vinz could only feel a sort of cold comfort knowing that he had finally managed to get through to Elor the only way he could; the panther's hurtful, manipulative streak had finally caught up to him.

"At least let me stay another night," Elor said, in a soft, sad voice that suddenly showed his true feelings.

Damn that cat, Vinz thought to himself. He had no reason to show any compassion or pity toward Elor any more. Why did he find it so hard to just tell him no?

"Don't worry, I will," Vinz said lowly, his voice echoing the same feeling of despair. *But please go tomorrow. Don't you dare give me time to change my mind*, he added silently to himself.

* * *

The next day, while Elor searched for a place to stay, Laz came over to Vinz's flat and the two began a long, painful discussion. As the wolf explained that he couldn't bring himself to share his lovers no matter how much he wanted to make amends, the fox could only nod sadly.

"Having Elor around really did throw a spanner in things, didn't it?" Laz said, his face in his hands.

"I'm not sure that's how I'd say it," Vinz said, turning away, as if he would turn to stone if Laz's eyes met his. "It's just that... I think you'd be better off with him."

Laz looked at him sadly, imploringly, as hurt and bewildered as ever. "Why?" was all he could manage.

"He's clearly got more of what you need, whatever that is," Vinz said, a hint of bitterness in his voice as he looked in Laz's direction but gazed past him.

"Are you jealous?" said Laz, stepping into Vinz's field of view, forcing their eyes to meet. "Vinz, wolfy, please, I still love you."

The imploring gaze was too much. Vinz began to sob and growl all at once. "That's enough," he said. "Stop tearing out my heart, fox! I want no more of you!"

Laz stepped away for a moment, tail curled and ears back

with fear.

"You made your choice, so go run with that carousing cougar all you want!" Vinz continued.

Laz stepped closer to him, reaching out to place a hand on the wolf's shoulder. "But Vinz..." he began.

"Go!" the wolf growled sharply, twisting away from Laz's hand and pointing at the doorway.

Laz slunk away sadly, looking as forlorn and vulnerable as a little orphan kit as he made his way out of Vinz's flat and across the shanty town to his little crate in the far corner of the hold. He closed the curtain, lay down on his mattress, and began to weep bitterly.

Of all that had happened to him, from the time his family discovered his fondness for males to the day he fled the surface after losing his job and home, this was by far the worst day of his life.

The heartbroken fox silently begged whatever gods would listen to bring the day to a close as he cried himself to sleep, feeling utterly helpless for the first time in many a year.

* * *

Elor, meanwhile, was gone for almost a full day, and everyone wondered where he'd gotten off to. He still had things at Vinz's place he needed to move, Laz was in desperate need of comfort, and Bram and Alrie were more than a little worried.

When the panther finally showed up again late that evening, Laz was the first to see him. The fox perked visibly as he saw the panther's familiar shape come through the curtain and sit down beside him.

"Elor! We were worried about you," said Laz. "What kept you so long?"

"Just had to make a few deals is all," said Elor. "I've managed to get a new place, one of the safest in all the ship. It'll be just us and one neighbor, other than that it'll be an entire hold like this one, all to ourselves, with the entrance to the hold guarded by the Cylinderheads' meanest guards."

Laz's eyes went wide. "When can we move in?"

"Tomorrow night, if you want," said Elor, taking Laz's hand and kissing it delicately.

"May I come too?" The two turned to see Bram standing in the doorway of Laz's crate, looking somewhat nervous.

"I don't see why not, we can make space... but why do you want to come too?"

The otter looked away and fidgeted, his fingers tapping on each other. "I... er... There's a lot I haven't told you about me. I need to get somewhere safe first, though."

Elor nodded. "Understood. We've all got secrets that can kill us here. Meet us at the Cunning Little Vixen tomorrow night, and don't worry about your things, they'll be taken care of."

* * *

The next evening, as Vinz dressed for work, two very scary-looking creatures, a coyote and a ferret, walked right into the flat and began grabbing Elor's things.

"Hey, wait! What are you doing?" he shouted, clearly outraged that anyone would simply walk in like this.

"A moving job," said the ferret. "Mr. Kaya wants this stuff delivered, and we don't say no to Mr. Kaya."

So Elor had flunkies to do his chores now? Unbelievable. The wolf let them work, all the while fuming that Elor didn't have the courtesy to hire creatures with some manners.

* * *

As the night drew on, Laz, Bram, and Elor met at the Cunning Little Vixen and stepped inside. A Cylinderhead guard nodded to Elor and opened the discreet door at the back of the bar area. Down the long steel ladder and back down another corridor, they found themselves in the holds of sublevel 6.

"The lower cargo hold," said Laz, surprised. "But how did you manage to get a place down here?"

"It helps to have Kerro Hemini's favor," said Elor.

They walked through the hold. There wasn't a great deal of cargo, though a few new items had been added since Elor had been there last; among them some boxes of typing supplies, a crated engine for an Invicta Cub biplane, and a chassis cab Star-Lutra Squire, a popular medium-duty truck. This one was tagged for export and had left-hand steering, probably waiting to be picked up by a Lycocian heavy cargo transport.

"There are only two entrances to this hold, the freight elevator and the service entrance," said Elor.

"Hardly anyone ever comes here. The shipping company controls the elevator, and the service entrance, well, we control that," the panther said with a knowing grin. "Ah, here we are!"

Next to Kerro's converted engine crate stood two more large crates, discreet doors added to their structure. Elor pulled out two sets of keys. "These are small, but they're well-hidden and very safe. I had them wired for electricity, and lined with 12mm-thick steel in case someone gives us trouble. I've even added a few touches I think you'll enjoy."

He handed one set of keys to Bram, who opened the door of his crate and was amazed at what he saw. A very clean, modern living space awaited him, with art-deco trim aplenty. A scheme of white and jade green ran throughout, with polished aviation-grade aluminum trim. A brand-new television set and sonigram player sat in one corner. "My sincerest thanks," he said with a warm grin. "Good night, you two... pleasant dreams!"

"Now let's take a look at ours, shall we?" Elor said with a grin. With that, he opened the door. A pleasant, comfortable home in a very traditional style awaited them. White walls, polished wood floors, an oak four-post bed, and a small table filled the space. The sonigram player and television sat near the bed, though somehow even with all this, the space looked spacious and inviting.

Once the door was closed and locked behind them, Elor took a seat on the edge of the bed, suddenly looking heartbroken. "Laz... I can't do this. Do you really know what you're getting with me?"

The fox sat down beside him, looking worried as he leaned

in close. "I'm getting a smart, handsome, confident lover who cares about me, aren't I?"

Elor could only return a sad sigh, shaking his head. "All my life that's what I've wanted to think, but foxy, I'm no good. I was bad to Vinz and I deserved to lose him. All I've ever done is use him, then hurt him when I didn't get my way. And now... now I make my living at the expense of others' lives. I'm just a selfish, spiteful pile of lies, Laz. Is that what you want?"

"That's not what I see," said Laz. "You're not perfect. You've made mistakes, you've done things you shouldn't have. But Vinz hasn't exactly been perfect either. He's so insecure, he thinks if I even look at a handsome fellow it's the end for him. I love him, but he'd rather push me out of his life than share me with you. He's not looking for a lover, he's looking for a worshiper, because if someone isn't groveling at his feet for affection he thinks he's worthless."

Elor looked Laz in the eye, practically nose-to-nose with the smaller fox.

"Just promise me something," he said.

"Anything," Laz replied.

"If I'm ever as bad to you as I was to him, don't take it from me. Get away and find someone better."

Laz nodded. "I will. But I will pray every night that I never have to."

The two embraced, kissing deeply, Elor's strong hands caressing Laz's lithe frame. For some moments they froze just as they were, then Elor got to his feet, stepping over to the sonigram player and opened the cabinet underneath. He looked through his collection of tapes, searching for the perfect one, and pulled the wide acetate belt out of its protective cardboard tube. He slid it over the felt-covered tensioners inside the player, then let them go tight, careful not to let the tensioners pop too suddenly and break the fragile tape. He pressed a button on the console and the tape reading heads moved into place.

Elor strode up to Laz as a soft, old-time waltz began to play.

"Shall we?" he said, bowing politely.

"I would be delighted," the fox said with a gentle smile as

he got to his feet.

With that, the two waltzed about the room, Laz feeling like he was dancing on air. He was safe, and with a handsome, virile, and wealthy lover who cared the world about him. This was true, unquestionable bliss and he wanted to savor the moment for as long as he could.

An hour later, as the last of the waltzes faded to an end and the sonigram player's heads snapped loudly away from the belt to reset themselves, the two sat down on the bed, nuzzling each other warmly and unbuttoning each other's shirts.

Elor then slid off his trousers and the linen shorts underneath and leaned in to kiss Laz on the neck.

"I'll give you anything you want... anything," the panther said, gently moving the fox's hand under his tail, to leave no doubt what he was implying.

"Ooh... That does sound like something I'd want, very much," said Laz, pulling off the rest of his clothing as he and Elor fell back into the soft, luxurious satin sheets of the wide, warm bed.

Elor lay back, spreading his legs wide, an almost feminine come-hither look on his feline features as he looked up at Laz.

The soft light from the torchier in the corner made a soft halo around the fox's russet fur, his handsome form that much more radiant as he leaned forward, planting a passionate kiss on Elor's muzzle.

How lucky am I? Thought Laz, maneuvering his hips between Elor's legs and pressing forward, sighing blissfully as fox and panther melded into one single being.

They lay there, Laz taking his time, thrusting slowly in and out of his lover with Elor holding him close, his legs wrapped tightly around the fox's hips.

Neither wanted the moment to end; they wanted it to last all night long, and Laz found himself easing off as the pleasure only tingled more intensely in his well-buried member.

For three blissful hours they mated this way, neither's gaze straying from the other, neither's body ever breaking the intimate embrace, until at last the pleasure finally overwhelmed

Laz completely.

He pressed his knot into Elor for a final time, the white-hot climax making him see stars as Elor clenched obligingly, lovingly around the base of that swollen bulge.

They lay together, intimately joined, until at last Laz's body relented and they were once again free... Only for Elor to give Laz an encouraging lick. The fox needed no more hint, and they made love once again, the world fading away around them as the pleasure consumed them completely.

Neither was sure exactly when they fell asleep; their intimate bliss faded seamlessly into the gentle haze of a dreamless sleep as the night wore on, their passionate lovemaking seeming to never truly end as sleep at last found them.

CHAPTER ELEVEN
The Mystery of Lt. Malga

A jackal, wearing the uniform of a Nightwatch agent, made his way down the corridors of the Imperial Air Force headquarters in New Lycopolis. The agency had just found evidence that pointed to shocking new turns in a vexing mystery that the Air Force thought they had solved nearly two weeks before. But more than that, it pointed to an astonishing link with a case the Nightwatch had been working on for almost as long.

The agent found the frosted glass door leading to the Department of Investigations and opened it, walking directly to the Chief Inspector's office and entering without so much as a knock. "What is the meaning of this?" bellowed the Chief Inspector, an aging tabby cat whose face was always fixed in a look of indignance.

The agent simply flashed his badge, pulled out a paper evidence bag and set it onto the inspector's desk. "We've got some serious evidence you should probably see. It seems our missing Agent Hollax and your missing Lieutenant Malga might have some connection. Ready a conference, and get your best agents in on this."

"Lt. Malga is dead, inspector," the cat growled at him.

The agent shook his head. "That's what you think," he said.

The Chief Inspector sighed heavily, shifting uneasily behind his desk. He pressed a call button on a small desktop speaker. "Ready the conference room quick as you can, we've got an emergency meeting. We need all personnel on this one."

A few minutes later, the agent, the Chief Inspector, an Air Force colonel, and several high-ranking field agents from both the Nightwatch and the Department of Investigations all crowded into a small, sparsely-furnished conference room. The lights were turned off and a projector was switched on, its small electric fan spinning up to speed as a portable screen was set up and pulled into place.

The agent spared no niceties and cut directly to the point. "What we have on our hands is nothing short of the strangest case I have seen in all my days. It seems that the cases of Agent Hollax and Lieutenant Malga may be inextricably linked, but frankly the more we learn, the more confusing this gets."

At that, he pressed a button on the side of the projector. Its first image appeared, a well-lit staff photo of Agent Hollax.

"Klai Hollax, serial number SP7698912. A Nightwatch agent in good standing for five years. Impeccable background. Our records show his life and family history is very well-documented. Vanished 9 Lai."

He clicked the button again, advancing to a slightly less formal photo of an otter posing confidently next to a Star Javelin interceptor.

"Lieutenant Bram Malga, 103rd Interceptor Wing based out of Morillia. Serial number IG49453. Deserted during a routine sortie over Tartús, last seen over Basecraft Cirrostratus. Presumed, according to Imperial Air Force reports, to be dead. Now here's the interesting thing... We can't find anything about him. All his papers on file were forged. He somehow managed to live under the noses of the Nightwatch *and* get into the Air Force on bogus records. There is absolutely no legitimate record of his existence before enlisting. What's more, we haven't the faintest idea who he actually is. Not a single dossier in our records on any citizen or foreign national even comes close to matching his description."

There was a hushed murmur from everyone in the room,, particularly from those with the Bureau of Investigations. The Imperial Air Force had been seamlessly infiltrated by an unknown agent with a made-up identity. This represented a monumental blunder on the part of the military... one that would not sit well with the emperor.

The agent continued. "Since the disappearance of Agent

Hollax and Lieutenant Malga, an otter vaguely similar in appearance to one or the other has been seen on several occasions in and around the holds of the Basecraft Cirrostratus."

The agent clicked to an image of an otter, turned slightly away from the camera, talking with a fox just outside a sausage stand.

"He was first assumed to be our own agent, having changed his appearance and defected in the line of duty, until our agents discovered this."

Rather than clicking the projector again, he put on a rubber glove and reached into the paper bag he'd been carrying. He produced a green, unlabeled bottle, the sort that most often contained bootlegged beer.

"This was found outside the hovel where our primary suspect had been living, and recovered by one of our field agents. Analysis of the fingerprints confirms that the prints belong to none other than Lieutenant Malga, meaning the body recovered from the site of the wreckage of his plane was most likely Agent Hollax. However, since the military in their infinite wisdom decided to incinerate his remains, we will probably never be able to confirm this. I just hope the High Command has a damn good apology for our departed agent's relatives."

There was another hushed murmur, this one decidedly more restless and tense.

Several creatures were seen to fold their ears back in annoyance... most notably those who represented the Imperial Air Force. The Nightwatch had just made fools of them all.

The agent continued his presentation. "As you all know, the murder of a Nightwatch agent is the one crime for which Emperor Salaar has given us infinite jurisdiction, and we were about to arrest Lt. Malga when we lost sight of him on 15 Lai. He was last seen in the company of two other creatures going into the notorious Cunning Little Vixen."

The projector was advanced to show a slide with two photos, side by side, of a young fox and a middle-aged panther.

"The fox is Y'Lazde Malek, known affectionately as 'Laz,' formerly a technician at the airship yards in New Lycopolis, age

28 years. Wanted for various crimes of perversion including unnatural and unholy acts and seducing a government official. The cougar is one Elor Kaya, formerly a professor at the University of Highridge, age 38 years. Wanted for Indoctrination against the Imperium, antisocial activity, sedition in speaking, unnatural and unholy acts, and owning an improperly licensed kitchen knife. We suspect one or both may have been directly involved in this conspiracy, but neither have been available for questioning since vanishing along with Malga. One of our informants, a member of the wait staff at The Vixen, questioned Vinz Nivariya, a known compatriot of Malek and Kaya. Nivariya had nothing helpful to offer; we don't believe he knows where they are, and doesn't seem particularly interested in knowing."

At this point, the inevitable question came up, from the Chief Inspector himself. "Is this some sort of all-male sex ring, then?" he asked. "Maybe Malga was one of them, trying to infiltrate the military."

"You and I have access to the same records. Malga showed absolutely no deviant tendencies whatsoever," the agent replied. "None of the details add up, and no one who could possibly tell us what's going on is available for questioning."

"Then why are you telling us?" a lion wearing the stripes of a first-order general asked demandingly.

"I was hoping that the Air Force might actually know something we didn't, being related to your investigation and all," the jackal replied with a hostile glare. "Though I see that was too much to ask."

"That's quite enough!" said the chief inspector, very annoyed at this agent's barbs at the military. "We only work with what we know, and given what we knew I think we have acted with impeccable judgment thus far!"

The jackal narrowed his eyes at the feline inspector. "Well then, what does the military's impeccable judgment tell you to do about all this?" he said, holding up the bottle and waving it in the cat's face.

At this point, the colonel, a coyote who had sat quietly and stoically throughout the whole meeting, at last spoke up. "We'll do what we always do when the enemy's not engaging. We're going to raise hell and flush them out."

At this, a middle-aged wolf, one of the field agents for the Bureau of Investigations spoke up. "But how do we flush them out? Won't we just flush out everyone else on the basecraft along with them? We already know the creatures involved are experts at losing themselves in crowds. It might take hours of interviewing everyone before we got them."

"Then we get them in some sort of scenario where we can detain everyone," the jackal replied. "You all know full well that most of the oceanic class basecraft circle just outside the jurisdiction of our investigative ministries. We can investigate, but we can't prosecute. It's only a matter of getting the basecraft into national jurisdiction... properly over land instead of seven kilos away from shore, for instance... and we can move in and arrest every single one of those miscreants. I think a mass execution of fugitives from the Cirrostratus would send a very clear message to the rest of the reprobates in the realm."

There were nods and murmurs of agreement. Then the wolf spoke up. "But we can't just have the Cirrostratus' flight plan ordered to change. Too many things depend on the ship being on her usual rounds, and any deviation would raise alarm immediately."

The coyote spoke up again. "Then maybe arrests won't be necessary. Supposing we... arranged for an 'imminent threat' on board the basecraft that made it criminal for us not to shoot her down? You wouldn't mind too much if your suspects went down in flames, would you?"

The jackal shook his head. "I couldn't care less. As far as I'm concerned they all deserve to die. If you can find some reason to blast that den of lawlessness out of the sky once and for all, I'm with you, damn the investigation. We all know Malga's guilty of something, don't we?"

The coyote leaned forward. "Good, because we're going to need the Nightwatch to help us with this one."

It took a long consultation with several top Nightwatch inspectors and several top-ranking ministers in both the Ministry of Civil Aviation and the Air Force to convince Emperor Salaar to approve the proposed orders.

Shooting down the Cirrostratus, an investment of billions of Crowns and a symbol of pride for his regime, was a tall enough order; creating an elaborate conspiracy to justify shooting it down in the first place was an even harder sell.

"I can't believe I'm approving this," the emperor said to the assembled cadre of top advisors as they sat around a massive marble conference table deep within the Imperial Offices in New Lycopolis. "If not for all the headaches these misfits have caused me lately I would have sooner let them live out their miserable lives cowering in the steel belly of that basecraft."

"The Imperial Air Force thanks you," said a badger in a deep blue uniform with black piping.

"Your thanks will not be necessary, Minister Vinyon," the emperor said coldly. "I... do what I must do, nothing more. Well then, if we have no more business?"

"Nothing further, Your Excellency," several of the assembled creatures murmured.

"Very well. Let me be, I have some things to attend to," the emperor said, standing and turning his back to the assembled ministers. They filed out of the room quickly and quietly, leaving the emperor gazing at the wall.

When the last of the creatures had left the room, Salaar turned to make sure the door was closed, then picked up the chair he had been sitting in, dashing it against the hard marble table, sending it splintering into several pieces.

He then took a deep breath, straightened his suit, and pressed a call button on the wall. "Send an attendant to conference room B, one of the chairs has collapsed. Then ready my car, I'll be returning to Lutrum immediately," he said.

"Right away, Your Excellency," a voice crackled across the speaker.

He left the room, shuffling furtively toward the vast garage where his motorcade waited, wondering, for once in his life, if he had finally gotten in over his head.

CHAPTER TWELVE
Peril from the Sky

From time to time, the Basecraft Cirrostratus' reserves of K-39 would run dry, and it would pause midway along its route and travel a few kilometers to the south.

There, moored to a tall tower, sat a tanker similar in shape to the Cirrostratus but a good measure smaller and with fewer facilities. Its only inhabitants were a crew of about a dozen or so workers who would help maneuver the heavy hoses and couplings to the pumps as the basecraft came in about 100 meters above them. The whole thing would take several hours and the basecraft would often drop substantially in altitude as it took on the enormous weight of several million liters of K-39.

One such refueling day came on the 21st of Lai. Elor, who had thankfully not been sent on another job since the incident with Hannock, had decided to sleep in late. He and Laz had been awake most of the night up to their usual antics, and now lay clutching each other, contented and oblivious to the world around them.

The sounds of the refueling were just enough to make them open their eyes or twitch their ears from time to time, but neither seemed bothered at all. Their minds were as far from the hoses and couplings as the puffy cumulus clouds high above them.

It was only as the process finished, with the Cirrostratus rising in altitude and turning back to its route, that they realized something had gone horribly wrong.

From out of nowhere, there was an almighty crash from the front of the ship, one that shuddered throughout the hull and sent creatures falling from their seats.

The ship's airframe groaned loudly as the entire basecraft

listed hard to the right, upsetting several buildings in the shanty town and causing Laz and Elor's home to slide several meters.

It held this way for a full minute before settling upright once again with another deep groan. The ship's engines could be heard outside, straining against the sudden torsion, and throughout the narrow corridors of the hull, alarm buzzers sounded.

Above, in the hotel and club decks, a voice calmly announced on a loudspeaker not to be alarmed and that the situation was being taken care of. But far below in the holds, there were no such reassurances, and creatures ran every which way as pandemonium set in.

The first creature to try to get a grip on the situation, not surprisingly, was Kerro. He immediately began putting out the word with his Cylinderhead allies that he needed to know what the commotion was all about.

The Cylinderheads, of course, had their own interest in protecting the basecraft and were no doubt already fanning out across its length and breadth, trying to find out exactly what went wrong and if possible aid in fixing the ship.

Laz, Elor, and Bram had each dressed themselves hastily and staggered upstairs to the Vixen, where total chaos had set in. A fennec waiter was trying to put out a small fire that had started in the corner of the room. A leopard with a Cylinderhead patch on his jacket lay sprawled on the floor bleeding from an ugly head wound, apparently dead. Papers, trays, bottles, plates, and chairs lay everywhere, and creatures ran to and fro, trying to fix what they could.

Kerro walked by just as the three were almost to the exit and clutched Elor, looking at him with a panicked expression. "Elor... It's the gyro!" he shouted. "They've taken out the gyro! We're headed for the mainland!"

As Laz heard this, his heart sank. The massive ship had a pair of fins at the rear, set underneath the hull at a 45 degree angle to the flight deck, but these alone weren't nearly enough to steer such a heavy craft.

Early on the engineers at the airship works had figured out a clever solution: a 7 meter-wide gyroscope, a massive steel wheel weighing in at more than 50 tonnes and mounted on a gimble. This was the heart and soul of the massive ship's steering system; without it, the Cirrostratus may as well have been just another hot air balloon.

Something in Laz's expression changed immediately. His normally carefree look was gone, his muscles taut, his normally twitchy ears bolt upright and alert. Something deep within his being had switched on with a loud clank and a sudden flash, like a gas arc searchlight ready to scan the skies.

He turned to Elor, a purposeful look on his usually soft features. "I need to go," he said, "I'll explain later." With that, he bolted for the stairway to the upper decks as fast as he could.

Before Elor could say anything, Vinz stumbled by, a bloody but luckily minor gash in his arm staining his shirt and a terrified look on his features. "I can't find her!" he said to the confused panther, grabbing him and shaking him hard.

Elor put a hand calmly on the wolf's shoulder. "Vinz... You can't find who?" he said in a firm voice, looking him straight in the eye with a calm expression.

"It's... ah... erm... Alrie... Can't find... she was here... went running... We have to find her, Catts!" Vinz was clearly on the brink of tears, half-hysterical and panting hard from panic and exertion.

Bram and Elor looked at each other. "The gyro," they said in unison.

Alrie had a keen interest in all things mechanical and chemical; it was only a hunch, but it seemed the most likely place to find the curious young ferret.

"Elor, you may want to go with Vinz. I'll stay and see if anyone down here needs help," said Bram.

"Right," the panther said, taking Vinz by the arm and heading toward what he could only guess was the general direction of the gyro.

* * *

Some distance away in Highridge, a television crew waited on standby.

It was all neatly planned out; an air traffic station on the Isle of Sighs would be watching its monitors, waiting for the signature of a basecraft to pass a certain pre-determined point nearing the mainland. An advisor from the Air Defense Command would then give the television crew a call, and they would travel to a press room on the grounds of the Imperial Palace.

There, they would set up their equipment for a live press conference as Emperor Salaar read a pre-prepared statement.

As far as the public would know, the Basecraft Cirrostratus had been hijacked by an unnamed rebel group and turned straight toward Highridge, where the rebels intended to set off a large cache of explosives in its holds.

Immediately following this announcement, a detachment of interceptors would be sent to shoot down the basecraft before it could reach the mainland.

Nobody knew exactly when the call would come, but they knew it was about to happen. Everyone on the television crew could clearly see that something about this didn't add up, that it all looked like a staged performance, but no one dared make their reservations known. Staged, dramatic announcements like this were commonplace, and questioning them only led to more trouble than it was worth. They were there to do a job, nothing more or less.

A low-slung, streamlined bus converted into a mobile broadcasting unit was loaded with equipment outside the Imperial TeleRadio building in downtown Highridge, then there was nothing left to do but wait and listen.

* * *

Something stirred within Fil Barron that he had not felt in years. It was more than a simple sense of impending disaster brought on by the ship shuddering and listing violently. This was something he'd felt before, years ago... a premonition that some tragedy loomed over the fates of innocent creatures, and every fiber of his being called him to seek out that creature, whoever they were, and protect them with his life.

He had only felt this once before in his life and paid the price for ignoring his intuition. Now charred timbers and painful memories were all he had left.

The kind-hearted dreamer of so many years ago was gone. Hate and fear had destroyed nearly everything he once was. He himself had killed many times, annihilated entire families, trying in vain to silence the memory of his loved ones' anguished cries by avenging them.

All that was left of his humanity was the single, burning desire to prevent the death of even one innocent, for once in his wasted life. Revenge and senseless violence could never put his soul at ease; only preventing another needless death would bring him the solace he had sought for so long.

Taking a crude machine gun of his own design and slinging it across his back, Fil went where his intuitions carried him, out of the shanty town in the holds of the Basecraft Cirrostratus for the first time in many lonely years.

* * *

To say that Elor, Laz, Vinz, and Alrie were bemused to all find each other standing on the catwalks that surrounded the massive gyro would be an understatement.

They weren't alone, either; several of the Cylinderheads' best mechanics were there too, trying their best to free the seized wheel.

Even more surprising to Elor and Vinz was the fact that Laz seemed to be supervising, and that Alrie was taking a very active role in the repairs. When they arrived, the plucky young ferret was sitting on a much larger tiger's shoulders, her smaller hands ideal for reaching the bearings they were inspecting at that moment.

Laz turned to the wolf and panther. "Looks to be sabotage... it doesn't look good either. There's no sign of any of the ship's crew down here, they should have responded ages ago but we can't even get anyone on the internal telephone," he motioned to a dial-less black phone receiver resting on the wall.

"The bearings are seized, we're still looking at it but it looks like someone poured grit or something into the lubricant sump. Would have seized them within a few minutes."

"How do you know so much about the gyro?" Elor asked.

"I was part of the crew that built this assembly, Elor," Laz said. "Didn't I tell you? I used to work at the Imperial Airship works."

"You mean you didn't even know what he used to do before he came here?" Vinz said.

"Does it matter?" asked Elor.

"It might have been good to get to know each other, before you started fucking and all!" the wolf growled.

"Enough!" Laz shouted. "I have had just about enough of you, Vinz! You can be so petty and selfish. Why don't you take a look around you and get your head around things for once? This isn't about you, wolf. We're all in big trouble and there's no one to help us so either give us a hand or fuck off!"

Just then, Alrie pulled her hand free from within the bearing housing, her arm fur matted and nearly black with grease. "If there's a spare bearing around it'll be an easy change," she said. "A few hours, not much more."

"There should be, check that metal case there," Laz replied. "If whoever did this only poured a bit of grit into the bearings they really underestimated us."

At that, another of the Cylinderhead mechanics, a marten in leather trousers wearing a bandoleer strap full of large-caliber bullets over a dirty white undershirt, came down a ladder from one of the upper levels of the catwalk. "You might want to take a look, fox. It's not going to be that easy."

As Laz scrambled up the ladder, Vinz and Elor looked up through the steel mesh floor to try to make out what was going on in the relatively dim light.

"Oh shit!" the fox shouted as he reached the top of the ladder.

Before him lay a devastated mess of electrical wires, hydraulic fittings, and control panels smashed beyond recognition... along with the bullet-riddled body of one of the ship's technicians.

"What is it, Laz?" Vinz asked.

"The entire control unit's been fucked to the Desert of the Damned!" Laz replied, his voice cracking in exasperation.

Laz climbed back down the ladder, a look of dismay and disgust on his features. "Looks like they took a hammer to the controls. Whoever did this wanted to disable the ship just enough to get us moving the wrong direction. All across this ocean there are military outposts that a civilian craft would be shot down for flying over. Not to mention the mainland, where most of us have the death sentence already. I'm not sure what direction we're heading yet, but With no control over the ship we're bound to fly over one or the other. Whoever did this wanted an excuse to blast us out of the sky."

"The Cirrostratus won't get shot down, mate," said the tiger on whose shoulders Alrie had been sitting. "We got planes an' we got guns, an' not a one of us can't take on the best interceptors the imperial forces' got to offer. We'll take 'em, won't we boys? It's Victory By Blood!"

"Aye! Victory by Blood!" each of the Cylinderheads shouted in unison.

It seemed about the thousandth time Elor was quietly glad to have a ruthless gang of savage underworld thugs on his side... though he had his doubts that they could really take on the Imperial Air Force. They had to be good pilots and good fighters, but they lacked the discipline and technique of a trained military force. If nothing else, they'd provide a brief diversion and hopefully buy them some time.

The Cylinderheads began to leave the catwalks around the gyro... presumably heading up to the hangar deck to ready their planes, or to alert the others.

Laz shook his head sadly as Alrie wiped her hands on an already oil-soaked towel. "The only way to stop us from flying over military airspace might be to get to the bridge and steer by throttle. We might be able to use the rear stabilizers to help, too. I suspect that might only buy us a few precious hours by flying in circles, though."

Vinz nodded. "To the bridge, then," he said. "Elor, can you do me a huge favor?"

The panther looked his way. "Yes?"

"Take care of Alrie for me," he said. "Take her down to that lower hold, and don't let anything happen to her. Stay with her until we're all safe and if anyone comes near her, blow them away," the wolf said.

Elor nodded. "I will. Be safe, Vinz," he said.

He hesitated a moment, then suddenly threw his arms around the bemused wolf, holding him tighter and more warmly than he had in many, many years. "I'm so sorry..." he said.

"For what?" Vinz asked.

Elor thought about it. For all he had made of it in the past few days, the wolf really had gotten over him years before. If he apologized for not joining him in the holds when he still had the chance, he was really only apologizing to himself.

"Nothing," he said sadly. "We'd best be on our way." With that he gave Alrie a nod and the two turned to walk away.

Vinz and Laz followed, and the four exited the gyro housing, trudging back toward the middle of the ship where they at last parted ways. Vinz and Laz went up the stairs, while Elor and Alrie went down.

Elor looked back as Vinz and Laz made their way upward. *I wish you knew what I'd meant*, he thought sadly.

CHAPTER THIRTEEN
The Wounded Cirrostratus

Up on the bridge, Laz and Vinz's worst fears were realized.

The navigator and flight engineer both lay slumped over their stations, blood pooled around their lifeless bodies. Each had been shot in the back, multiple times as if the shooter had been less concerned with killing them and more concerned with making a cruel sport of it- a trademark of a Nightwatch assassination.

The pilot, communications engineer, and captain were nowhere to be seen; perhaps they had managed to get away safely.

On their climb through the levels of the basecraft, Laz and Vinz hadn't seen a single other creature; it seemed most of the passengers and crew had been quickly and neatly evacuated. It seemed the only aircraft left in the hangar deck that didn't belong to the Cylinderheads were small passenger planes and a few larger craft damaged when the ship had rolled.

On the flight deck, not a single plane remained; it seemed every large airliner and cargo plane had been co-opted in the evacuation efforts.

Laz pushed the lifeless form of the flight engineer out of his chair and looked over the controls before him. "The plan is to steer by throttle control," Laz explained. "If I can throttle down the starboard engines that will leave only the port engines pushing us along. We'll end up flying in an enormous circle but at least we won't crash... or fly over military airspace."

"Why not fly somewhere friendly?" said Vinz.

"Like where? Lycocia?" Laz said. "Not likely we'd get clearance. Besides which they're under treaty to return fugitives.

What do you think we'd be if we arrived in a stolen basecraft?"

Vinz rubbed the side of his head, squinting his eyes in frustration. "You realize what this means, then. One way or another, they'll get us. We're only buying time," the wolf said sadly.

Laz's ears sagged, his mouth slightly open and his eyes downcast. "Isn't that what we've been doing since we came here?" he said. "All we've done since we arrived in this blasted ship is buy time. We shouldn't have even survived this long."

Vinz's first instinct was to clutch Laz to him and beg him to be his again, but he thought better of it. If they survived, then they'd go about the business of reconciling. Until then, there was only one sentiment that he thought could convey the gravity of the situation. "Then we'll go down together, you and I" he said.

Laz nodded, his strength seeming to return. He sat up straight in his chair, then reached for the two levers that controlled the massive compound radial engines on the Cirrostratus' starboard side.

He powered them down to the lowest possible speed they would run, but decided not to stop them completely. Laz had worked mainly on steering systems and although he didn't know much about the engines, he knew if they stopped, starting them again wouldn't be as simple as turning a key, pulling the choke, and advancing the throttle.

"See what you can pick up on the radio," Laz said. "Any bulletins about us, any public news broadcasts, anything... it might help us know what our chances are."

Vinz nodded, running to the radio and flipping the switch. The console dials lit up, a gentle electric hum and that peculiar smell of heating vacuum tubes emanating from the large radio. The wolf had never used such an advanced radio before, but the knobs weren't that much different from one of those high-end world band sets a civilian could buy. He set the reception band to short wave, the preferred signal for dispatches and bulletins, and began to turn the tuning knob, hoping against hope to find some signal that would tell them where they stood.

Rose LaCroix

*   *   *

Bram, meanwhile, sat at a desk in a darkened studio, a single light on his face and a camera pointed at him. He fidgeted with his hands somewhat- something he seemed to notice himself doing more often these days- then decided it would be best to rest them on the desk, folded together thoughtfully.

In the confusion below decks, he had quite literally run into an old acquaintance. He was a wolf named Lyko Funai, a communications officer who had deserted from the 103rd Interceptor Wing just months before Bram, and both were astonished to see each other. After only half an hour discussing the situation, the two hatched a plan- desperate, but definitely worth trying.

"Are you ready?" Bram said.

"Everything's ready to go. I'm surprised Salaar's boys didn't smash this up on their way out," Lyko said.

"Good job they didn't," said Bram. "We'd be trying to do this in semaphore. Alright, we go live in 3... 2... 1..."

*   *   *

A white-tailed stag, an aide on the imperial staff, ran panting through the halls of the Imperial Palace near Highridge. The emperor had just given his announcement about the supposed hijacking of the Cirrostratus and was in no mood to be bothered, and the stag knew he might catch hell for it. But this was important.

A pair of uniformed guards brandishing machine guns recognized him as a trusted individual and saluted, allowing him to enter the chamber where the emperor paced restlessly amid opulent oak and marble accents.

A sonigram of a gorgeous aria sung by a tenor vocalist played in the corner as the wolf paced his chamber. He was about to lose the Cirrostratus, the empire's first and finest basecraft. A billion crowns in building costs and perhaps another quarter

117

billion in revenue would be lost in only a few short hours.

But he was bound to his word. Dogmatism was his faith and his way of life; it had to be so because he had to be firm and fast. What would his subjects think if they couldn't count on him to be hard and fast to his own word, right or wrong?

Just then, the aide burst in.

"Your Highness... I have some... bad news," he said, flinching.

"Bad news? Well on with it! Don't snivel in your emperor's presence!" Salaar snarled.

The aide said nothing, only walked over to the console of the sonigram and switched it to its onboard radio. A voice crackled through the roar of static and the whine of a heterodyne- a voice that sounded vaguely familiar to the emperor, though much older and more confident than he remembered.

"...the atrocities perpetrated on the people of Tartús were far worse than anything state news agencies have reported. On the day I deserted from the Air Force, I was sent to bomb an orphanage. That day, I knew I would rather die than continue to live in fear. I am deeply sorry that I allowed this tyrant to bully me out of power, young though I was I should have stood up to him and not fled for my life, cowering and living incognito. But now I ask you, people of Greater Lutrovulpes, if you will have me, if you will forgive me for having failed you, then I shall gratefully accept the restoration of the monarchy. I want nothing more than to restore the constitutional monarchy of our own nation, and the sovereignty of those subjugated under the hateful regime of Minister Salaar Avys. If our allies in Lycocia are listening, I beg that you will grant asylum not only to myself, but to all the creatures who live in the holds of this basecraft and grant us clearance to land. There is scarcely a single soul here who does not deserve..."

Salaar reached for a pistol kept in his vest pocket and shot the console, fangs bared and a feral growl emanating from deep within his chest as the now-silent machine arced and sputtered.

"How many channels is this on?" he screamed, grabbing the stag by the collar.

"All of them, Your Excellency," he said. "Short wave, long wave, radio, television even. He's using the signal jamming hardware we had installed on the Cirrostratus."

The emperor's jaw went slack. He himself had specifically ordered these signal jamming stations on every basecraft. It was meant to be a measure that would allow these primarily-civilian craft to be used by the military as flying bases in a national emergency, but its presence had been a secret and its design state-of-the-art. No one had counted on anyone on the basecraft even knowing it was there, let alone figuring out how to use it, and it had seemed like a waste of time for Salaar to order his agents to sabotage its controls.

Now this hardware had been used against him, and by the last creature he had expected; the last of Salaar's reservations about shooting down the Basecraft Cirrostratus were suddenly gone.

In moments he was on a direct line with the Ministry of Defense.

"...That's right, all television and radio. Jam them! We don't want this bastard saying anything more... Yes, I'm bloody well aware that half the world's already seen this broadcast. Just do it!" He slammed the receiver back on his desk telephone, breathing hard, sitting down at his desk with his face buried in his hands.

Suddenly he pointed to the door. "You... Get out!" he shouted to the stag. He obeyed, closing the door politely behind him.

Salaar slumped at his desk, gazing at the floor in shock and dismay. He could only hope the refugees on the Cirrostratus didn't find any of the other military hardware hidden in its massive hull.

* * *

Back on the bridge of the Cirrostratus, Vinz and Laz too had heard the broadcast. Bram- make that King Brannagh IX- had finished his broadcast before Salaar's orders to jam the signal had gone through, and now everyone with a radio or television for perhaps a thousand kilometers or more had seen or heard it.

"Well now... That explains a few things, doesn't it?" said Vinz, genuinely surprised. The otter had always been coy about his background, but it all made sense now.

"So... he was right there all along, hiding right under everyone's noses," Laz said. "Salaar must be mortified."

Vinz nodded. "Seems you've smoked ghella leaves with royalty, fox," he said playfully.

"Indeed... Wait until Elor hears about this!" Laz replied.

The wolf shook his head, suppressing a growl. He was still not happy with Elor.

"How's our heading?" asked Vinz, hoping to change the subject.

"Hard to starboard, circling nicely," Laz said with a smile.

Just then, a speck appeared on the horizon. At first it appeared to be a large bird, or a single plane. It closed fast-too fast. Suddenly the single speck revealed itself to be several specks, each one growing fast as it closed, heading straight for the bridge.

In only seconds Laz could see that it was a flight of Star Javelin interceptors. "Get down!" he shouted.

Both ducked instinctively behind the control consoles just as a hail of 20mm bullets ripped through the bridge, blasting the stuffing and springs out of the chairs they had been sitting in only moments before. Only the thick steel of the outer bulkhead on the far side of the control consoles saved them.

"I thought the Cylinderheads were going to help!" said Vinz. "They must have been caught off guard," said Laz.

"Laz... I have to ask you something..." the wolf said, a terrified look in his eyes. "Are the gas bags filled with hydrogen?"

"No, it's always been helium, the Cirrostratus was the first to have it" Laz replied calmly as they walked quickly toward the door leading into the stair wells to the interior of the ship.

"Wonderful... so instead of roasting in a ball of flames we'll die in a mess of twisted metal and sea water," Vinz said flatly.

"We're not going down without a fight," said Laz. "Follow me, I've got something to show you."

CHAPTER FOURTEEN
The Battle

Down on the hangar decks, the Cylinderheads scrambled to prepare their planes, hastily checking them for damage from the basecraft's roll some hours before. They had been caught unawares, and now they had to somehow get all of their fastest, best-armed planes to the deck without catching fire from the detachment of interceptors when they came by on a second strafing run.

The four large elevators worked overtime getting planes to the deck. Brightly-colored craft, some civilian monoplanes with armament and some stolen former military craft, painted shades of yellow, blue, and blood red with the distinctive skull-and-propeller symbol of the Cylinderheads on their tails began to crowd the deck. The pilots rushed to get them into the air as quickly as they could in the lull between strafing runs, dividing the main runway into halves and taking off from both ends of the ship.

No sooner had the last of twenty of these planes left the deck when the air force detachment returned, more bullets ripping into the wood and steel atop the basecraft.

Suddenly, the interceptors found themselves surrounded when at their midnight and 9 o'clock positions came two flights of 10 planes each, their guns blazing. The Star Javelin's main weakness was its horrendous glide angle when disabled, and it showed; four of the thirty or so Javelins went down immediately, their engine blocks cleft open by a spray of relentless fire.

The remaining 26 air force fighters broke formation. This wasn't just a matter of strafing a lumbering basecraft any more; the mission had become a fast and dirty dogfight, the first one most of the pilots in this detachment had ever experienced.

The cylinderheads, meanwhile, showed their expertise in aerial combat. Not only had most of these pilots been in dogfights with rival gangs, but a few of the more seasoned Cylinderheads were former air force pilots themselves. They knew all the tricks the air force could pull and how to head them off, and even behind the controls of slower and less agile planes their fierce defense strategies shattered the expectations of the terrified air force pilots.

Planes went every which way, streaking over, under, and alongside the basecraft in a dizzying, lethal dance. By the time the air force had scored their first kill among the Cylinderheads, they had already taken heavy losses; only eight of the original detachment were left in the air.

Then it was seven; the eighth pilot grossly misjudged a dive and smashed his plane violently into the stern end of the Cirrostratus' flight deck. The craft shuddered as 25 tonnes of alloy and high-grade K-39 splintered through the end of the wooden deck and ignited in a deep-orange fireball.

With incredible precision, a Cylinderhead deck crew scrambled to the scene, turning fire hoses on the flaming wreckage and working to clear the deck as quickly as possible. For them, it would be a particularly long night; the skirmish was taking its toll and they would have to tend to wounded pilots and damaged planes when it was all over... not to mention refuel the planes that were still airworthy.

With the deck cleared, the remaining 16 Cylinderhead planes were moved into position as their comrades in the air took on the last five of the air force interceptors. They were never needed; the Air Force wing commander ordered a retreat, and the surviving five pilots left as quickly as they had arrived.

There was subdued celebration as the Cylinderhead fighters touched down on the deck of the Cirrostratus. It seemed the worst was over; a gang of thugs had taken on some of the best-trained pilots in the world and won.

In a small corridor just below the level of the flight deck, however, the celebration was muted as Laz and Vinz made their way to a row of stations on hydraulic lifts. Vinz immediately recognized them as 25mm anti-aircraft guns, the sort one would normally see on a battleship or on a battery like the one protecting Archer's Cove.

"I wasn't even supposed to know they installed these," Laz said as he ran his hand down the long, gray-painted steel barrel of one of the massive guns. "No one was supposed to know, except maybe a few trusted workers. But you know how it is in a shipyard. Hard to keep secrets. Used to play cards with the crew who built these... never could keep a secret, that lot. If the Cylinderheads can't hold them off, we'll give them a little help."

"But it sounds like the air strike is off, we probably don't need them now," Vinz said.

"Don't be so sure, wolf," Laz replied. "Let's stay here. At the first sign of trouble we'll each take a station. Press the red button on the console to your left to raise the gun to deck level, use the hand cranks to aim, You know the rest."

A tense hour passed as the two waited, each able to hear the other's breath as they sat next to each other, ready to spring into action at the first sign of trouble.

Suddenly, an alarm shrieked through the corridors, red lights flashing and sirens blaring.

The hairs on Laz's neck stood up. "That's our signal, one of the Cylinderheads must have figured out how to sound the alarms. Come on!" he shouted.

With that Laz pressed a button. The gun station rose quickly, flipping open a concealed hatch on the edge of the flight deck. Vinz followed, and they began scanning the skies for any signs of the Imperial interceptors.

Suddenly, the air was alive with a swarm of craft coming in from every direction. "Fire at anything without the skull and propeller!" shouted Laz.

The two began shooting every which way, tracer rounds illuminating the late evening sky. Immediately, three interceptors were hit, and the air force fighters were caught so off guard that it gave the Cylinderheads a chance to scramble a few of their own fighters.

They will get us eventually, Laz thought grimly as return fire from one of the interceptors ricocheted of the thick steel shield on the front of the gunning station. Without some last moment reprieve, this was the last of their borrowed time and everything would end in a final terrifying moment of bloodshed.

But Laz, Vinz, and the Cylinderheads had no choice now; this was their fight, and it was time to do or die.

* * *

The phone rang, and Salaar reached with a weary hand to answer the call. On the other end of the line was Jaigon Klanar, head of Dai-Yel Petrochemical... and he was quite irate.

"I thought I told you I wanted Alrie Wenna alive!" he shouted. "I need to interrogate her! There's a leak in my plant. You can do anything you want with the others but don't kill that girl until I've gotten everything out of her I can!"

Salaar was not happy to hear this. "I already told you, I'd made up my mind. She's just another troublemaker, Jaigon, you'll have to find that leak on your own," he replied.

"I don't care if you are my cousin, I won't stand for this!" Jaigon screamed. "What she knows could bring down the empire!"

Salaar's blood boiled at the very suggestion that his cousin- his inferior in status- would even attempt to change his mind. "All the more reason to kill her and the rest of those ill-begotten misfits!" he shouted.

"You will be sorry," Jaigon said.

Both hung up at the same time, Jaigon slamming his receiver with such force that the brittle black plastic shattered into a thousand pieces. This was the last straw; Dai-Yel Petrochemical was far too important to the empire for its interests to be treated this way.

Salaar couldn't abuse him or his interests this way any longer; the day had come for Jaigon Klanar to collect his due.

* * *

What Jaigon didn't know was that Salaar hadn't even planned to wait until the Cirrostratus was shot down to get rid of Alrie.

In a move to deliberately spite his irritating cousin, Salaar had sent four Nightwatch agents after her; the same four Nightwatch agents that had failed to catch Elor Kaya. Now they were faced with an ultimatum: they could choose to be disgraced from the ranks and sent to be worked to death in a steel mill, or to take part in a suicide mission and receive all honors as commissioned agents upon their deaths, including a healthy death benefit for their families.

For agents of the Nightwatch, who were expected to value honor over all things, there was never any question.

They had searched everywhere for Alrie, but found no sign of her in the usual places. They could only go on a hunch that she was probably in the company of Elor... wherever he was.

It was as they were searching the shack that Laz had formerly called home- now toppled and splintered from the ship's violent shaking earlier- that they found a matchbook for the Cunning Little Vixen. It told them nothing, but with no other leads to go on they decided to search the bar itself.

The bar had previously been off limits to Nightwatch agents; it was usually heavily guarded by Cylinderheads. While the basecraft was under attack, however, the vicious thugs that normally flanked every doorway had their hands full up on the flight deck. This meant that every doorway within The Vixen was open to them, each and every one.

Elor peered through a small peep hole he had made in the door of his home. He'd heard voices, and thought it might be Cylinderheads looking for Kerro. His heart sank when he saw the dark trenchcoats and bowler hats of four Nightwatch agents. His blood ran cold when he realized they were the same agents- a wolf, a fox, a ferret, and a marten- that he had seen once before, shouting and cursing on the apron as his plane left the ground.

So... they're still after me, Elor thought to himself.

"Get down, get out of sight," he whispered to Alrie. She did as she was told, crawling under the bed and into the surprisingly small space inside the box section beneath the mattress. For once, she was thankful for her slight build; hiding inside the bed might actually work.

Elor, meanwhile, opened a wooden chest sitting innocuously at the foot of the bed. He pulled out all of his guns and loaded each of them as quickly as he could. He stood staring right at the door, and waited with bated breath as the Nightwatch agents grew closer and closer.

Alrie was terrified. There were thick steel plates protecting the room, but if they had armor-piercing rounds or if the Nightwatch got inside, there would be nothing but a down mattress to protect her; all she could do was hope against hope that she would neither be found by the agents nor shot accidentally if they did manage to get inside. There was nowhere to run, and only Elor and his makeshift arsenal to protect her. She began to sob quietly, knowing full well that she might not live to see her sixteenth birthday.

Reaching for a pen and a scrap of paper that lay on the floor beneath her, she scrawled out a quick drawing and climbed out long enough to hold out her hand. "Elor... If they get me, take this."

Elor turned for a moment and walked toward the bed, reaching down and taking the scrap from the terrified young ferret. He opened it up and looked down, confused at first.

There before him was a complex chain of hydrocarbons. From his schooling in biology he knew this was no organic matter but something synthetic, though not unlike petroleum or methane.

"K-39," Alrie said.

Elor could only nod in astonishment. "K-39. This explains everything," he said.

K-39... the life blood of the Great Wolven Imperium. The synthetic fuel was the country's chief export, the one great bargaining chip with democratic powers like Lycocia, and the one thing that made aviation the world over cheap and accessible.

At only 1 to 3 Imperials to the liter, it was far cheaper than any naturally-occurring fuel. If some foreign power managed to get their hands on the formula, it would mean any respect the world had left for Salaar's heavy-handed regime would be lost.

"That's why I can't go home," the terrified young ferret said.

"But how did you figure it out?" asked Elor. "That's something chemists the world over have been trying to work out."

She looked at him, a quizzical look, almost as if he were asking her how she knew the alphabet or how to count. "I don't know, I think I saw it in a book somewhere. Or maybe it was something they had written on a wall. I don't know... I just... know, I guess," she said.

Vinz had been right. Alrie was a genius, a rare sort of accidental genius that soaked up knowledge from anywhere and everywhere even if she never could recall where it was from. If she knew the formula for K-39, Alrie probably knew so many things that could bring Salaar to his knees.

But she was more than that; Alrie was a gentle, shy and sensitive soul and a young one with so much of her life ahead of her.

Elor went back to the doorway, waiting for the agents to come as he slipped the small piece of paper into his vest pocket, over his heart. "I'll hold onto this, Alrie, but they're not going to get you. I promise."

CHAPTER FIFTEEN
Lycocia Calling

A gray cat paced his office floor restlessly, his tail twitching behind him. Never in his whole career had a predicament like this presented itself; it was the sort of dilemma that could make or break a career in politics.

Word had spread quickly about the situation aboard the Basecraft Cirrostratus. Although his television and civilian-band radio signals dissipated somewhere over the vast Eastern Ocean, the short-wave signals that carried King Brannagh's plea for help were picked up as far away as the east coast of Lycocia.

From there, the press took over. Newswires were sent via teletype and telegraph, and telephones at all the major news bureaus began to ring off the hook. Now Jord Lak, Prime Minister of Lycocia, was caught in the middle of one of the biggest controversies of the decade.

Prime Minister Lak shook his head. *They don't have this trouble over in the GWI, do they?* For once a state monopoly on media sounded like a good idea to him. But then, didn't it sound good to anyone with a few sins to reckon with?

If you control the flow of information, you can control the world. But ruling the world wasn't in the cards for Jord Lak. He was an elected official, and for all the pomp and circumstance of his career, he was just another civil servant.

PM Lak had been voted into office on a free trade platform; the time, he said, had come to allow the world marketplace to ply its goods in Lycocia so that Lycocia could ply its goods to the world. His opponent, Zida Sol, had run on a protectionist ticket.

When Zida Sol had denounced Emperor Salaar's government

as corrupt and oppressive, Jord Lak's campaign was able to play it up as a potentially damaging remark. Lycocia relied on the Great Wolven Imperium for, among other things, K-39 to keep its vast numbers of private cars and planes running; Sol's protectionist mindset, they said, would cripple the country.

The voters were convinced and punished Sol at the polls. Jord Lak won by a landslide, 64 to 32, with the remaining 4% going to an assortment of fringe candidates.

In Lak's first month in office, tariffs were slashed and Lycocia's ports were opened wide. A great deal of negotiation with Salaar's regime took place, resulting in a treaty that allowed both nations to waive tariffs in exchange for a policy of non-aggression. One of the clauses in the treaty required Lycocia to return all fugitives to the GWI, and that no requests for asylum from the GWI made upon entering Lycocia would be granted.

By far and large, Lak had support for these policies. The average opinion in Lycocia about Salaar's regime ranged from total indifference to smiling admiration; anyone who talked about the regime's draconian laws and its use of kangaroo courts and summary executions was generally looked down upon as being on the idiot fringe.

But it seemed things had suddenly changed. The public reaction to the news had been swift, and within a couple of hours there were no fewer than a thousand protesters outside the gates of One Executive Place, the Prime Minister's residence and office. The signs they bore all carried the same clear message: ASYLUM FOR BRANNAGH.

There was more to the dilemma than just the public reaction, however. As several popular news reporters had astutely pointed out, the treaty with Emperor Salaar specifically stated that requests for asylum made at the port of entry would not be honored. It said absolutely nothing about requests for asylum made before entering the country; this cross-band radio and television address had been made from international airspace.

Even so, it wasn't as if Lak could just grant asylum for King Brannagh and the refugees of the Cirrostratus without expecting repercussions. Although it was well within the terms of the treaty, it might be seen as a gesture in bad faith. Salaar could withdraw from his end of the treaty, and may even impose an embargo. All the diplomatic work PM Lak had done in in the first five years of his term would be destroyed in one fell swoop, and he wouldn't likely be re-elected when his six year term ended next year.

He paused and sighed, his tail twitching restlessly, and looked out the window of his office. The office window looked out on an open plaza formed by the two executive buildings flanking One Executive Place, and faced the open side of the square, beyond which lay a mile of manicured park lands filled with national monuments. Across the square now, spilling out into the park lands and even climbing the monuments, more and more marchers came, each with the same demand.

Jord Lak turned away from the window, letting the red velvet drapes fall silently over the panes of glass as he let out another long sigh. Even if he did save face and managed to keep the treaty alive, he would never be re-elected by these people; not after sending a much-loved king and hundreds of innocents to their deaths.

Suddenly he heard a commotion over the sound of the marchers and ran to the window. A sleek black limousine with Lycocian flags mounted on either side of its tall radiator grille plied its way toward the gates, moving slowly through the protesters.

They parted reluctantly before it, shouting and glaring angrily through the car's bullet-proof windows. Inside sat four of PM Lak's cabinet ministers. Lak was glad to see them; it would give his staff time to put heads together and reach a decision about the refugees on the Basecraft Cirrostratus.

Though to Jord Lak, the answer already seemed clear.

* * *

It was close to sunset when the phone rang yet again in Salaar's personal office. An aide, the stag who had brought the news of King Brannagh's address earlier that day, was seated near the doorway.

Across the vast office he could only hear a few of the muttered words of the emperor and see his expression fade from one of rage to one of complete despair. "I see..." Salaar could be heard saying. "We'll discuss this another time."

With that, the emperor hung up that phone, then picked up another one next to it: the direct line to the Ministry of Defense.

"This is Emperor Salaar. Tell Air Minister Vinyon to Call off the Interceptors and await further instruction on the Basecraft Cirrostratus," he said. "And end the signal jam on the Cirrostratus' communications."

He hung up again, then sat at his desk, looking the most defeated the stag had ever seen him.

"Come here," Salaar said to his aide in a voice that could barely be heard. The aide approached timidly, and waited patiently for the emperor to speak. "Send word to Press Minister Dathur that we will allow the Cirrostratus to land in Lycocia, and that the Lycocian government has agreed to repair and return the Cirrostratus. We will then negotiate the possible return of our fugitives in exchange for their safe arrival. This will not affect our treaty with Lycocia in any way."

Salaar was genuinely crestfallen. He had finally lost his nerve, giving in to compromise and diplomacy.

He sat back in his seat, face in his hand, slumped, disheveled, and sweaty. "Don't waste my time, go!" he said to his aide... though not nearly as emphatically as before.

*   *   *

The sun had very nearly set on the Basecraft Cirrostratus and, it seemed, on the lives of the few creatures who lived there. A third wave of fighters had arrived, lighter and faster planes than the Javelin interceptors before them, and the Cylinderheads had begun taking more and more losses. Vinz and Laz still sat at their gun stations, tracer rounds streaking just inches from their faces as they fired back at the planes hurtling down from the sky like avenging furies.

"We're almost out of ammunition," Laz said. "It's only a matter of time."

Suddenly, the planes stopped shooting, and began to pull away. In the fading light the fighters could be seen turning away and lining up in tight formation before banking sharply. Off into the night they flew, away from the setting sun into the darkened east.

"It's a trick, it has to be," Vinz said, ears swiveling warily.

Laz was completely silent and barely moved a muscle, only his eyes and ears moving as they scanned the darkening skies for any sight or sound that would confirm their worst fears.

The long wait began, both creatures convinced that another attack was imminent. They sat breathlessly at their gun stations, the evening chill at their high altitude finally starting to sink in.

Laz was starting to shiver. "I think we should take these down below decks, Laz," he said. "They'll sound the alarm if they need us. Besides, we wouldn't want to survive this only to freeze to death, would we?"

Vinz nodded stiffly, activating the lift and letting his gun station lower back into the much-warmer hull of the Cirrostratus. Laz followed suit, and the two stepped away from the gun stations. They huddled together in the corridor, keeping each other warm as they held their long vigil.

*   *   *

Down in the holds, Elor made his last stand against the four agents. He had spent all the rounds in both pistols, firing tit-for-tat through the peep hole at the agents, who seemed to have been armed with a great deal more ammunition... or perhaps they had managed to find some in one of the crates.

At last, he looked down at Alrie, still cowering beneath the bed. "Whatever happens, be good for Vinz," he said. He took a deep breath and racked the Gyram machine gun, ready to burst out the door, firing until he ran out of bullets.

He ran to the door, pushing it open with his shoulder, and immediately began to lay down a volley of fire. The Nightwatch agents dove for cover, but before they could return fire another gunner opened up on them. Instead, they turned their fire on this other lone gunner.

Elor knew this was is chance. He ran back inside and slammed the door, just in time to feel a spray of bullets thumping against the thick steel behind him as the holds erupted in a furious explosion of gunfire.

It all lasted only a few tense moments; one last errant shot rang out, then all was deathly quiet once more.

Alrie and Elor waited a moment for any sign that the fire fight might continue, then stepped out the door cautiously to survey the scene.

An acrid cloud of gun smoke lingered heavily in the air, clouding the scene. Alrie coughed slightly as they looked around, waiting for the smoke to clear.

There lay the four Nightwatch agents, dead as any creature could be, but there was no sign of their mysterious rescuer.

"Let's go... we're not safe here any more," said Elor. They made their way toward the stairway to the upper hold.

"Look," said Alrie as they made their way through the hold.

There, behind the rear of the Star-Lutra truck, lay the body of Fil Barron.

Elor knelt by his side, tears welling up in his eyes. He took Fil's hand in his own, looking down upon him sadly.

"The last man on Earth," he said, looking at Alrie. "Gone."

The last of a dying breed had given his life to save a child he never even knew.

But to Fil, no such profound thoughts had ever crossed his mind. To him it was only a chance to make right. When the children of his village had needed him, he was far away and did nothing.

What difference did it make that this child wasn't a human like himself? Alrie was still a child by any measure.

Mumbling a prayer in the old feline tongue- the first he had said in perhaps twenty years- Elor closed Fil's sightless eyes and folded his hands upon his chest. He knelt his head in reverence as he mumbled the prayer again, then folded his hands in silence as Alrie looked on, stunned and speechless.

At last, the panther stood. "Come on," he said, suppressing a sob. "Vinz and Laz might need us."

* * *

Just moments later, as Vinz and Laz huddled in the darkened corridors next to the gun stations, their bated breath flowing in tendrils in the growing chill of the night, and as Alrie and Elor made their way through the wrecked slums of the upper hold, a very disagreeable sound filled the air.

It was the dreadful whine of microphone feedback, and it was coming from the ship's public address system.

"Attention please, all creatures on board," a voice said.

Vinz, Laz, Alrie, and Elor all immediately recognized it as King Brannagh's voice.

"Jord Lak, The Prime Minister of Lycocia, has just granted us safe passage into Lycocian air space. Salaar has agreed to this and called off all air strikes against the basecraft as of 2100 hours. All creatures aboard will be considered for political asylum in Lycocia. In a few hours a detachment from the Lycocian Air Defense Force will arrive. They will have passenger liners to shuttle us to the mainland, a light cargo plane carrying mechanics to help repair the ship, medics to help our wounded, and a detachment of interceptors to help escort us safely. They should be arriving by tomorrow morning at the latest. For those who helped us, I want to thank you. Especially my friends Y'Lazde and Vinz." A cheer went up from every creature who heard this announcement.

Vinz looked at Laz, his head cocked sideways. "You never told me your proper name was Y'Lazde," he said.

Laz could think of a couple of things he could say in response to that, but decided not to sour the mood; he would deal with Vinz's jealous double standards later.

CHAPTER SIXTEEN
Fallout

Night fell on Highridge, and with it a restless peace descended across the world. It was not a lasting peace; it was the sort of quiet that falls upon battlefields immediately after a cease-fire, a tense and unnatural quiet, tinted with notes of perennial anxiety and sepulchral finality.

Emperor Salaar sat at his desk, eyes wide open and bloodshot, his form slumped. The beleaguered emperor had been seated there, scarcely moving an inch since his aide had left. He could not, for all he was worth, bring himself to leave his office and go to sleep.

He had gone soft. He had given up. He had failed as supreme leader of a state that he, himself, envisioned and created. He felt like a father who had watched his child fall into a ravine and done nothing: weak, irresolute, and worthless.

He glanced at the small, stainless-steel desk clock across from him. It read midnight, and it felt like it took an eternity for the thought to register in his tired mind.

No sooner had he wrapped his mind around the concept of what time it was when his office door burst open. Jaigon strode in, his eyes on fire with vengeance. Several of the guards who had previously been guarding the door and corridor entered with him, along with a compliment of high-ranking cronies including J.M. Huurin himself, the leopard retail magnate who owned most of the stores and newsstands across the GWI.

"I have a score to settle with you," Jaigon said, his lupine muzzle turned in a predatory snarl as he pointed forcefully at the emperor. Two of the guards then rushed forward and seized Salaar, dragging him to the floor.

"What are you doing? Let go!" Salaar shouted, resisting the guards furiously as they frisked and handcuffed him.

"Your time as emperor is over, Salaar," said Jaigon coolly, his murderous look replaced by an indignant scowl. "You're no longer fit to rule. Your mind isn't what it used to be. As the nearest living blood relative to the emperor I hereby demand that you be placed in custody pending a hearing on your state of mind, and that I become emperor in your stead."

"I'll have you all shot for treason!" Salaar screamed, straining at his handcuffs as the guards fought to restrain him. "I made you what you are today, and I can bloody well take it away with one stroke of the pen!"

"That's if we don't have you shot first, wretch!" J.M. Huurin shouted.

"We've been waiting for this day for a very long time," Jaigon said. "Oh, I admit, you were *very* good to us, but you never did give us what we really wanted. It was all token gestures to keep us on your side, to keep your war machine well oiled and your subjects in line. But since you were so kind as to give us a leg up, we thought we'd go ahead and help ourselves."

With that, Salaar was escorted out of his own office, kicking and screaming, to a waiting sedan. He was blind-folded, then shoved into the back seat and driven away at high speed to Jaigon's home some distance from Highridge.

Whatever fate awaited him at his destination, he knew, would be anything but pleasant.

* * *

Word of the coup spread slowly. When one runs a strict regime, it can go on running for some time on the pure momentum of fear and no one will notice that their leader is gone until they need new orders to act upon.

Not surprisingly, the military, who ran constantly on those orders, was the first to discover what had happened to Salaar. Although the Imperial Guard fell under the emperor's direct jurisdiction, the military had informants posted throughout their ranks, and the intelligence ministry kept a very close eye on their activities. When word got out that several guards had been involved in a plot to overthrow the emperor, word was immediately phoned in to the high command and an emergency session of the defense ministry was called.

The ministers sat huddled over a table in a secret room deep in the ministry headquarters, discussing plans to rescue the emperor. Air Minister Vinyon, in particular, seemed exhausted after the debacle with the Cirrostratus but remained an active party in the discussion.

Only a few short hours before sunrise, it was decided that the army would send a force to free Salaar, then await orders on what to do with Jaigon and his cronies... though it was already a foregone conclusion that a death sentence would be handed down swiftly.

They would move out at 1000 hours. The operation would be carried out by a large contingent of their most heavily-armed soldiers in broad daylight, hopefully shocking Jaigon into surrendering by the sheer audacity of the maneuver.

An order was sent out, and all personnel needed were put on standby to await further orders. The mission would be completed and the coup would be crushed before the day was done; the emperor would take his supper over Jaigon Klanar's dead body.

* * *

The sun rose on the Basecraft Cirrostratus that morning to find the deck covered in Cylinderhead planes, all prepared to take to the air once again at a moment's notice. Elor had watched them gather from the bridge, where he had been sitting since late that night. Vinz and Laz, meanwhile, had gone back to the holds to rest.

If I wasn't so sure they were dead tired, I'd swear they were down there making up... among other things, Elor thought. The terse animosity between the wolf and fox seemed to have melted away in the heat of battle, and both had curiously broad smiles when they went below decks. Not that Elor would have minded;

Laz was good enough to share, and he had become used to the idea even if it seemed a bit odd to him.

Now it was about time for them to come relieve him, to wait out the rest of the time until the technicians from Lycocia could arrive to help fix the wounded ship.

Elor heard someone enter the bridge, and turned, expecting to see Vinz or Laz. Instead, Kerro stood there, leaning rakishly against the doorway.

"You'd have made one hell of a hired gun, kid," said Kerro. "A few more hits like those two and you could've been a Cylinderhead."

Elor shook his head. "It was pure luck... and I hated doing it," he replied.

Kerro chuckled. "Never mind. I just wanted to talk for a moment, before some of us less... clean-cut creatures take our little exit. I've got a few things going on the Cumulonimbus that need looking over. Besides, it ain't likely Lycocia will grant asylum to the likes of us. Consider yourself lucky, you're getting off scot-free; you're invisible still."

Elor sighed. "Even if my hands are stained in blood," he said sadly.

"What's a stain here or there?" said Kerro. "Nobody's a saint, kid. Just keep a low profile and nobody will know. Though I advise you to watch your back... you've got enemies now. But I've got friends who can help you out. Anything you need, guns, money, a favor from the Lycocian parliament... and all you have to do for them is exactly what you done for me, read me chief?"

It was no sense saying no to Kerro; Elor gave him a cursory nod of acknowledgment, careful to keep his mouth shut.

"One more thing, I have something for you," he said. "If the heat is ever on and you need to get somewhere safe in Lycocia, you might need this."

He handed Elor a thick, plain brown envelope tied with a string. Elor opened it. Inside was a thick, hand-bound booklet with hundreds of names, addresses, and telephone numbers... and about fifteen thousand Lycocian Sola in bank notes.

"The money's just a little token of my appreciation... or

an advance on your next job, if I need you. That booklet has every safe house, every place to get cars or guns when you need them, every place to get good ghella leaves, and every one of my contacts in various... businesses," Kerro said. "Think of it as a sort of underworld phone book."

Elor stared at the thick stack of white paper, slack-jawed. "I don't know what to say," he said.

Kerro flashed his usual broad outlaw grin. "You're welcome," he said.

Below on the flight deck, the first of the Cylinderheads started their planes and began advancing toward the runway. "Well, best be on my way. This'll be no place for outlaws like me in a couple hours. Maybe we'll cross paths again," he said.

"Maybe so. Goodbye," said Elor, quietly glad to be rid of Kerro.

A few moments later, as Elor watched Kerro down below on the flight deck climbing into the cockpit of his personal autogyro- the rare Tannawani model he had seen when he first arrived on the basecraft- Laz and Vinz arrived to relieve him. Elor gave them both a polite nod and was about to head out.

"Wait!" said Laz. "I was thinking, Vinz should be alright keeping everything together until the Lycocians get here. And there's... something we haven't done in a good while."

"Oh, please," said Vinz, clearing his throat and trying to ignore them as he sat down at the throttle controls.

"Laz, I'd love to foxy, but I'm a bit tired you see," said Elor.

"Aww... too tired?" Laz said, a hand straying to the crotch of Elor's trousers and his muzzle just inches from the panther's, closing in fast and planting a kiss there.

Elor's eyes just went wide. "Maybe not," he said, suddenly feeling very spry as they ran down below decks to the lower hold.

"Damned foxes," Vinz muttered to himself.

As the two lovers left, all was quiet on the bridge. The Cylinderheads continued their exodus, the last one clearing the deck only an hour after the first had taken to the air. It was now close to 0800, and a bright, cloudless day had dawned over the basecraft as it continued its lazy circle somewhere about 140 km west of Archer's Cove.

There really was nothing to do here. With the winds relatively calm and blowing the ship westward at maybe one or two knots, and the controls holding a firm, easy circle, the ship practically flew itself. Vinz sat boredly at the controls, staring off into the distance, waiting for the Lycocians to arrive.

Suddenly, he felt a hand on his shoulder. He jumped slightly, then turned to see King Brannagh. "Your Mmajesty!" he said.

"Please... I was Bram to you from the start and I'll always be Bram to you," the otter replied.

"Well... how can I help you?" asked Vinz.

At that, Bram looked around the room to be sure there was no one else around. "I... well... In these basecraft... it's always been a place where a creature can... explore their moral boundaries, and... well, I've not exactly explored much. I mean that is... ahem... even a father of twelve might look at those gorgeous boys in the bars downtown with a wandering eye from time to time, right?"

Vinz was shocked. "Are you saying you want to...?"

"...Experience something decadent before we have to deal with Lycocian bureaucrats for the rest of our lives? Well, why the hell not?"

And for Vinz, there was no good reason not to. Bram was an especially attractive fellow in his own right, a slim, well-toned, handsome specimen of his species in the prime of life.

"This ship seems to be flying itself well enough without my help," said Vinz with a knowing grin. With that, the two headed toward the stairs.

"Let's go back to my place, that way we won't run into Elor and Laz," Vinz said.

"Wait," said Bram. "I have a better idea."

The otter darted toward the hotel deck, which had been totally deserted since the previous afternoon. In only minutes, the two had locked the door of one of the Cirrostratus' plush luxury suites behind them.

The two looked each other over nervously, then without

saying a word, began to undress.

Brannagh could barely believe he was doing this. If he ever says a word about this he's *dead*, the otter thought as he slid out of the red woolen thermal underwear he wore under his clothes.

He eyed Vinz, already naked. He was a bit paunchy, but for a wolf his age that was normal. He still had nicely-toned legs and arms, and a modest sheath between his legs. They both crawled onto the bed, looking at each other, sliding ever closer, neither quite sure what to do just yet.

Vinz saw his opportunity and seized it. He leaned over and began to gently nuzzle Brannagh's neck. The otter moaned slightly, his fur bristling at Vinz's advances.

Vinz ran a hand along the inside of the otter's thigh, holding him close. Brannagh's breathing quickened, but he didn't resist; he was uneasy, unsure of himself, and yet already the influence of his hormones had begun to take over.

If you're going to leave, do it now, his better judgment said to him urgently, but he could not bring himself to step away. Vinz had him, and it seemed the wolf, from his satisfied smile, knew.

Tracing his hand up the inside of his thigh, Vinz reached for the otter's sheath and began to massage it, a move that took Brannagh completely off guard.

The otter let out a sharp gasp and arched his back, not only from the pleasant sensations but from the sheer surprise of the moment. He felt a dizzying array of thoughts as he considered the source of this deft touch. Since when could a male do this? His mind wanted him to protest, to brush Vinz away, to deliver a knockout punch and then run, but his body didn't want to obey him. The wolf knew exactly how to caress just the right spots, and he was defenseless against his questing touch.

Brannagh finally gave in completely. He stretched out on his back, moaning, letting the wolf explore his body freely as his flesh crept out from its sheath, the cool air licking gently at its tip.

Vinz leaned forward and placed his muzzle against Brannagh's rapidly swelling member, giving the pink organ a long, slow lick around its exposed length, coaxing it further out into the open. The otter let out a surprised squeak followed by a satisfied moan as Vinz's tongue began to lap at him with a skill honed over many years.

The wolf kept up his pleasurable attentions, the otter resting a hand between Vinz's ears and rubbing softly as he bucked his hips. Brannagh closed his eyes, for the moment forgetting the how, why, where, and who of it all; with no sight to distract him all he had was the wet, silky expanse that lapped relentlessly at his shaft, the feel of a warm body nearby, and the curious scent of combined male arousal.

At last, Vinz paused for a moment, looking up at him with a grin. "Enjoying yourself?" he said.

Brannagh opened his eyes, then felt his fur bristle when he realized that he was enjoying the attention of another male- albeit a very skilled one- all too much.

He looked down at his shaft, coated in the wolf's saliva and a generous complement of his own precum. "Yes," he said, blushing visibly under his fur. "Yes I am."

"Good," said Vinz with a wide grin, taking Brannagh's shaft fully into his muzzle and suckling on it. The otter let out a huff of surprise and gripped the bedsheets as the warm, smooth sensation of the lupine muzzle and tongue drove a wave of pleasure through him. He closed his eyes once again as he began to thrust upward into the wolf's warm maw, losing himself.

Vinz bobbed his head up and down Brannagh's shaft skillfully for several minutes, the warm, broad expanse of his tongue very nearly bringing the otter off. Bram had begun to pant hard and Vinz was just about to let the otter explode into his mouth, but he suddenly stopped short. He pulled his muzzle ever so slowly off Brannagh's shaft, making sure to let as much saliva drip onto the otter's throbbing cock as possible before releasing it.

"Are you ready for a little more fun?" said Vinz, stroking the base of Brannagh's shaft. "Oooh yes," the otter replied. With that, Vinz lay down flat on the bed, lifting his tail. "A pleasure to serve you, Your Majesty," he said with a grin.

Brannagh sat up, taking in Vinz's physique. He was starting

144

to show his age a bit, looking a bit old for being in his early 30s, but Vinz still seemed quite a fine specimen... especially when he focused on the muscled back and tight, trim buttocks that lay before him.

He straddled the wolf, getting himself into position, but hesitated a moment... was he really going to do this? There was never any doubt in the otter's mind that he preferred females, and he knew this would change nothing. But his world had just been shaken; he had been taken aback by just how good this had been so far, and was starting to question what he knew about himself.

"Damn you for making me want this so bad... Vinz, if you ever tell anyone about this I'll bloody well kill you," the otter said as he began to grind the tip of his shaft under the wolf's tail.

Vinz looked back with a teasing grin. "Oh, I'll never tell," he replied, grinding back against the otter's rigid shaft.

At that, Brannagh could stand it no longer. He drove himself into the wolf and began to thrust as quickly as his hips could manage.

Vinz wasn't prepared for such an aggressive approach, and yelped slightly as the otter drove into him with such furious energy. For a species quite a bit smaller in stature, he was fairly well-endowed and every inch of his veiny, smooth shaft could be felt as it sawed back and forth into the wolf's taut entrance, its way eased only by a thin layer of saliva and precum.

Brannagh, meanwhile, was most definitely enjoying this. The warmth was familiar, but the tightness was exotic. Vinz certainly did his part by clenching at just the right moments, and the last of the otter's reservations about males fell in a smoldering heap. For the moment there was only flesh, fur, and raw body heat on his mind.

Brannagh's body let loose a furious wave of intense pleasure that shot from head to toe like an electric shock, his entire body going taut as a bowstring as he felt the indescribable tingle of sexual release throbbing through his shaft. He hilted into Vinz and let out a pleasured squeal, staying there for what seemed like an eternity.

At last, both wolf and otter began to release the coiled tension within their bodies. There was a soft sucking sound as he withdrew from the wolf and collapsed panting on the bed beside him, a streamer of cum tracing the trail of his still-hard cock as it took leave of its carnal sanctuary.

"Enjoy yourself?" said Vinz, sitting up and stroking his now-rigid lupine shaft.

"That was amazing," Brannagh said. "It was... I was... that was just as good as any female I've been with... otter or otherwise."

"You were... Mmf!... Quite good yourself," Vinz said as he began to stroke himself harder. Just then, he felt a gentle touch on his thigh and looked down to see Brannagh's hand there, petting and squeezing him.

"Here... let me help," he said. With that he leaned forward and, taking a deep breath, gave Vinz's flesh a long, slow lick. *Well, he did the same for me*, he thought.

Vinz moaned softly, then guided the otter's partly-webbed hand to his rapidly-swelling knot. The otter, sensing the cue, gave it a squeeze as his tongue brushed over the canine's tip, sending Vinz into paroxysms of pleasure. Hearing the wolf's pleasured moan, Brannagh continued this, intensifying his attention on these two spots and not letting go.

The relentless attention was too much for Vinz. The wolf let out a yip as a streamer of cum spurted from the narrow tip of his engorged member... all over the otter's face and into his mouth.

"Oh... terribly sorry," said Vinz, unsure of what the penalty for cumming in a king's mouth might be. Brannagh raised an eyebrow and spat out the peculiar-tasting seed. He paused, then wiped his face with the back of his hand as he glared at the bemused wolf.

"Remember what I told you, wolf," said the otter. "Not a word about any of this!"

CHAPTER SEVENTEEN
End Games

As planned, an elite detachment of soldiers stormed Jaigon Klanar's country estate that morning, detaining three servants and confiscating anything that could be used to seal a criminal conviction against Jaigon, including a bail of ghella leaves found under his mattress valued at over 4000 Crowns.

The heart of the operation, however, was a failure. When the soldiers broke down the heavily-bolted door to the basement, they found it empty, with clear signs of a forced exit. Emperor Salaar was gone, and a search party was immediately launched to find him.

Jaigon, meanwhile, was nowhere to be found and none of the servants in the house knew where he might be; it was assumed that he had anticipated the raid and fled to one of his four other houses. Nightwatch field offices across the Imperium were immediately phoned and a bulletin was issued, but Jaigon would never be caught.

Salaar, meanwhile, had escaped only two hours before the raid, around 08:00 in the morning. He had finally managed to cut through the 7mm thick shatterproof perspex windows of the first-floor room where he was kept... all the while wondering why Jaigon would have his house built with perspex windows in the first place. A broken candlestick was his only tool; using the jagged edges of the cheap metal he had finally compromised the dense plastic enough to break through it with his fists... after five exhausting hours of frantic scraping.

By the time the soldiers broke down the basement door, he was already some distance away, making his way along the narrow roads that ran through the rural east of the province of

The Goldenlea.

He knew that Jaigon's home was roughly midway between Highridge and New Lycopolis, but he decided against trying to go back to Highridge; after all, Jaigon or his cronies might be waiting for him there. He needed to get to New Lycopolis, to the headquarters of the High Command.

Even if his corporate cronies had turned on him, he could surely count on the military to come to his aid, couldn't he?

Salaar saw a car coming, the first he had seen in some time. It was a green Lutra Special, a design he had commissioned himself, and he had never been more thankful to see one. The tall wolf waved for the car's driver to stop.

The driver, seeing only a disheveled fellow who looked to be in distress, slowed down warily. A middle-aged ferret rolled down the window and leaned out, looking somewhat nervous.

"What's the trouble, then?" he said.

Without hesitation, Salaar lunged forward, opening the car's door. He grabbed the driver by the collar and flung him into a roadside ditch, climbing into the driver's seat.

"Your emperor thanks you!" he shouted, just before speeding off.

In the rearview he could see the furious driver getting to his feet and shouting as he drove on. Salaar suddenly found himself wishing he'd been able to silence the car's owner permanently; he now ran the risk of getting the police involved, and that would not necessarily be a good thing.

Salaar knew if the Nightwatch or Road Traffic Police got him, he would be recognized and released instantly; they answered directly to him.

If it was a local constable that arrested him, however, there was every chance that Jaigon and his cronies would get to him before the police realized that he was the emperor.

Then there was always the chance that one of his former cronies had the local police on payroll and would turn him in, even if they did recognize him.

Salaar wasn't about to wait around and try his luck. He pushed the little car to its limits, though he saw to his dismay that the 110 Km/h top speed he had specified in the design was proving far too slow. Suddenly, finding a Lutra Special didn't seem so lucky. He cursed his luck that the first car he had seen that morning hadn't been a Star Marellia tourer, or some overpowered, supercharged Lycocian roadster.

The road he was on, the R-296, was a rural road that meandered through forests for quite some distance before the next Hyperway access. Salaar could only guess that he was between 60 and 70 kilometers from the juncture of the H-71 and H-7, which would lead him to New Lycopolis and to safety.

He had been driving nearly fifteen minutes when he heard the distinctive two-tone siren of a police car and saw, in his rearview mirror, yet another Lutra Special painted in the East Goldenlea Constabulary colors of deep blue and yellow.

His heart sank; the situation was beginning to look more and more grim by the minute.

The road was starting to get more curved with the increasingly hilly terrain, and the little Lutra Special's tires squealed as he threw the car into ever-tighter turns at dangerous speeds.

The police behind him could barely keep up, the two tiny cars all-too-evenly matched on the treacherous curves.

A steep hill with a curve at its base loomed ahead, and Salaar braced himself as he threw the car almost suicidally into the tight turn at its base, the car spinning nearly 90 degrees and stalling. He was able to re-start the engine and take off just as the police came rolling down the hill, closing in on him every second.

He was only a short distance from the H-7 now, probably less than 45 minutes from the safety of the High Command complex where he would be recognized instantly.

A sign loomed ahead and he strained to read it as he passed it. He was just able to read out the legend "New Lycopolis: 40KM," and his heart began to pound. He was so close to safety, and yet so far away.

He looked in the rear view mirror. The police were hot on his tail now, though the gap seemed to never once narrow or widen when the road straightened. He cursed his luck once again that a faster car hadn't been available.

Salaar then realized that he'd been watching his rear view all too intently. He turned his attention back to what lay ahead of him, and felt a cold chill. There, straight ahead, were red and white caution signs indicating a sharp turn at the bottom of the next hill, and this time there was no time to brake at the last moment. Emperor Salaar cringed and waited for the inevitable.

PC Gil Burrock had chased suspects before, but he had never, in all his eight years with the East Goldenlea Constabulary, seen anything like this. The genet watched in horror from the driver's seat of his police cruiser as the suspect in the green Lutra Special tried to throw the diminutive car into a turn at more than 100 km/h, only to turn the car sideways, skidding at high speed across asphalt until asphalt gave way to grass. The car then began to roll violently, pieces of glass, body panels, and the car's canvas roof going every which way before at last the car smashed hideously into a thick tree and wrapped itself around its bough... nearly 200 meters from the road.

PC Burrock got out of his car and ran to the scene. What he saw confirmed his worst fears; the car was crushed so badly that the top of the roof line met with the level of the chassis at a pinch point about midway down the body. The suspect had been partly ejected through the car's roof and lay pinned between the tree and the car, his twisted, lifeless form just visible amongst the mangled wreckage.

Thus ended the bloodthirsty reign of Emperor Salaar.

* * *

Meanwhile, on the Basecraft Cirrostratus, the first planes from Lycocia, a converted civilian airliner painted white with the red Hannari oak of the medical corps, had arrived to shuttle the sick and wounded away.

Planes for the more able refugees were on their way shortly, then a small transport full of mechanics to fix the plane's gyro.

One last plane was on its way as well... this one on its way to collect the dead. There were 36 of them in all, not counting the Air Force pilot whose remains were charred beyond recognition, or any pilots whose planes had crashed into the ocean during the dogfight.

The Basecraft itself would then be flown to Lycocia's largest airship facility and completely repaired before being returned to New Lycopolis for recommissioning.

Vinz, Laz, Brannagh, Elor, and Alrie all stood on the hangar deck of the Cirrostratus, along with the rest of the basecraft's inhabitants. A few of the ship's crew, among them the communications engineer, had joined them.

He had survived the assault on the bridge because he had been in the latrine when the Nightwatch burst in and shot his crewmates. Upon hearing the gunshots and discovering them dead, he had fled to a closet in a disused store on the first sublevel and stayed there for several hours.

He was talking to Lyko, thoroughly impressed by how he and King Brannagh had managed to use the ship's broadcast and public address systems so effectively.

"I'd heard it was possible to broadcast on multiple bands with our equipment, but I never believed you could do a cross-band signal jam like this," said the engineer, a badger who couldn't have been more than 23.

"That's what those transponders were designed for," said Lyko. "They're built with the military's most advanced signal jamming hardware. I only knew about them from overhearing the commander discussing it with the Air Minister's office. In an emergency, Salaar and his staff would board one of these basecraft and run everything from the air, including doing regular radio addresses and holding cabinet sessions. I wasn't sure how it worked at first, but it wasn't that difficult once I sat down with it."

"Amazing what they hide in these craft without telling us," said the engineer, scratching his head.

"Did you see the anti-aircraft battery, then?" said Lyko.

"Is that what that horrible din was last evening?" the engineer asked.

Lyko nodded. "It was put to good use, yes."

Meanwhile, Laz strode up to Vinz and gave him a sniff.

"I smell otter on you, wolf," he said, affecting Vinz's serious demeanor.

"What of it?" said Vinz, his tone predictably defensive.

"Oh, nothing," Laz said. "You know, I've talked it over with Elor... you're welcome to stay with us when we get to Lycocia. In fact... I think we'd both like that."

Vinz sighed. He still had conflicted feelings about Elor, and doubted they would ever rekindle that long-dead spark. As for Laz, however, there was definitely something still there.

The ordeal of the previous night had only made it clear to him that he still loved the fox, and any opportunity to share a life with him was better than none. And yet, Laz didn't want to share his life alone; he had to bring Elor into the equation too.

Vinz frowned. The thought of Laz with anyone else was bad enough, but the thought of Laz with Elor made his jealous side white-hot with fury. Could he ever get used to the idea of sharing the fox?

But the only good answer to that, as far as the wolf was concerned, was that he simply didn't know. Only time would tell, and that meant giving the idea a chance.

He sighed, shaking his head a little. "We can try... I suppose," he mumbled.

With that, Laz leapt into his arms and kissed him repeatedly on the muzzle, wagging his tail. "You won't be sorry, you really won't!" he said.

Vinz glared slightly at Elor. "I certainly hope not," he said flatly, though his expression softened when he saw the joy in Laz's eyes.

They were such sweet eyes, framed in russet fur and lined in the gentle, almost feminine highlight of the dark skin of his eyelids, bright and radiant and catlike, and shimmering in even the dimmest light like slivers of onyx set expertly in amber. Oh, how those golden orbs sparkled when Laz was happy! Could he really, honestly say no to a face like that?

No, I don't think I will regret this, the wolf thought as they held each other in the shade of the hangar deck, the whole world momentarily forgotten.

* * *

Some hours later, Vinz, Laz, King Brannagh, Elor, and Alrie sat near each other on a Lycocian Air Force transport. Very few words were exchanged between them during the flight, only the occasional glance.

Laz, who sat between Vinz and Elor on the long line of webbed seats running the length of the fuselage, would squeeze one or the other's hand from time to time.

Each could think only of what lives would await them upon their arrival, and whether their stay as refugees would be permanent or if this was only a temporary reprieve.

Still, something told them that things had changed, and that they had somehow survived the very worst of it.

King Brannagh, meanwhile, leaned back and smiled contentedly. Sooner or later, he had to find some fitting reward for his friends... and perhaps another moment alone with Vinz.

There was no announcement made as the plane began its descent and landed at Dunham International Airport, on the east coast of Lycocia. It was the first of the transports to bring able-bodied refugees into the country.

The door opened as the plane came to a stop, and immediately soldiers began urging the passengers out, across the apron to a small building marked "Immigration." One guard took Brannagh aside before he could enter, escorting him to a waiting sedan that appeared to be armored, and drove him away.

The rest of them were jostled through revolving doors and brought to a lobby where a rope-marked corral created a snaking line to a row of makeshift desks; clearly, the Lycocian government had intended to get the refugees of the Cirrostratus processed as quickly as possible.

"Can you see what's going on?" said Laz to Vinz.

The taller wolf leaned forward, trying to get a view over the crowd. "They're telling some to go one way, and some to go another," said Vinz.

Elor pinned back his ears. This was exactly what he had

feared; one direction would lead them to a new life in Lycocia, and the other would lead them to some other fate... most likely, extradition and a swift execution on their return.

At last, the four of them arrived at a desk, and each declared their names. An immigration clerk, a rather old coyote who gazed at them through thick spectacles, checked their names against a list provided by the GWI embassy.

"Right, Mr. Malek, Mr. Nivariya, please step to your left, we'll have transport waiting for you. Mr. Kaya, Ms. Wenna..." he sighed sadly. "Please step to your right... I'm sorry it had to be this way."

"Wait, what?" said Laz.

Elor placed his hands on Laz's shoulders, trying his best to keep his composure. "Laz, don't," he said. "I... you're better off with Vinz anyway."

"But Alrie! She's just a child! Why are you doing this?" said Vinz, furious at the clerk.

"Vinz, don't jeopardize your own chances. Go, both of you."

"But Catts... why...?" the wolf sputtered.

Elor said nothing; he embraced Laz and Vinz warmly, fighting back tears. Alrie joined in the group embrace, clinging to the other three with wide, terrified eyes.

"It doesn't matter," said Elor. "I've loved you both greatly. And don't worry about Alrie. I'll protect her with my life if I have to."

Elor slipped Vinz a slip of paper. "Something from Alrie. It might be useful in getting us out of here. Take care of Laz for me," he said.

Their goodbyes may have lasted longer, but a mixed canine in a soldier's uniform broke them up.

"Come on, you're holding up the line, move along!" he said, pulling Elor and Alrie away. Another soldier jostled Laz and Vinz around a corner to a corridor, out of sight.

CHAPTER EIGHTEEN
Detained

Elor and Alrie were walked, silently and sadly, to the end of a long corridor. At the end stood a pair of double doors, wide open, and outside idled an olive green bus where a soldier brandishing a rifle motioned for them to get on board.

They were shuttled across the airfield complex to a disused military barracks facility, where they were to be held under armed guard until the Great Wolven Imperium arranged for their transport.

Without so much more than the shirts on their backs, the detainees in the barracks bedded down on stiff mattresses, laid down side by side in close arrangement. Only one semidetached building held the latrines and showers, and there were only ten of each to serve all of the hundred detainees in this particular building. At all hours an armed guard stood at either end of the vast room, with orders to shoot to kill if there were any attempts at escaping or signs of unrest. There was no privacy, no comfort, and no escape.

It seemed every day in those dismal barracks, Alrie clung to Elor, scarcely saying a word. Elor did his best to comfort the young ferret, though he knew it was all in vain. He was prepared to die and had accepted his fate, but it seemed so wrong to do this to Alrie. She was just a few weeks from her sixteenth birthday, and still very much a child in every way. Was knowing what she knew really so horrible that she deserved to die?

For some days they waited, each day tense and filled with grim anticipation. And yet, among those detained, a certain sense of solidarity began to form.

Gilyar Honyo, the filmmaker Elor had met during his first

night at the Cunning Little Vixen, had taken up a cot on Elor's other side, and over the next few days they talked for many hours. Elor told Gilyar nearly everything that had happened since that first night, and Gilyar, in return, opened up more to Elor than he had to any creature in many years.

One day, Elor remembered something. Of the few items he had brought with him in his pocket, one was an 8mm home movie cartridge. On some of his walks through the holds of the Cirrostratus, he had taken his camera with him and filmed, in as much detail as he could, what life was like for those creatures living in that underworld.

"If we ever get out of this alive, you might want this," he said, handing the pressed steel cartridge to Gilyar.

"What's this?" said the badger, looking it over.

"This is what may be the only record of where we've been," Elor replied. "The world we knew in those holds is gone forever now. If the world doesn't see it, they might never know it existed. I know someone like you will give this the respect it deserves."

"Thank you, my friend," said Gilyar, slipping the cartridge into his vest pocket. "Though you realize that the memory might die with us anyway. But until the day we die or become free, I will carry this close to my heart."

"And if we're freed...?" asked Elor.

"In that case, don't you dare lose touch," said Gilyar with a warm smile. "Not after what we've been through."

* * *

Laz and Vinz, meanwhile, had been taken to a hotel in downtown Dunham along with several other refugees who had been granted asylum. They were given four months to find a job and a permanent home.

Laz, however, wasn't thinking about jobs and homes; his thoughts were on Elor and Alrie, and how to save them.

"It isn't as if we can just march in there and get them," Vinz said. "They've got one of the most powerful armies in the world guarding that compound."

156

"Never mind that," said Laz. "There has to be a way. Really... doesn't anyone care about another creature's rights?"

Vinz shook his head. "The only rights some creatures care about is their right to have cheap fuel," the wolf said sadly. "As long as Salaar has K-39, Alrie and Elor are just bargaining chips to them. Wait a moment..."

Vinz suddenly reached into a drawer in the nightstand where he'd been keeping the contents of his pockets. He found the creased, crumpled slip of paper and unfolded it, his eyes going wide at what he saw.

"What is it?" asked Laz.

"The end of Emperor Salaar. Come on!" said Vinz, getting to his feet and grabbing his coat.

Laz followed behind as they left the hotel room, Vinz nearly running toward the exit.

"Where are we going?" he asked.

"The Ministry of Energy. They'll want to see this," Vinz replied.

Fully three hours later, after waiting two hours in the Dunham offices of the Ministry of Energy, Vinz was allowed to speak to a local representative.

The representative, a raccoon with a squeaky, nasal voice, looked over the slip of paper.

"What is this and why should I care?" he said, pushing his spectacles disdainfully up his nose.

"It's K-39," said Vinz.

The raccoon's jaw went slack.

"Is that so?" he said, looking over the formula again. It certainly looked credible; it was a complex hydrocarbon of some sort at least.

"I need you to see if you can get word to Prime Minister Lak about this," said Vinz. "Tell him there's no need to extradite the refugees from the Cirrostratus to the Great Wolven Imperium; Salaar can't hurt Lycocia if you know how to make K-39."

"All well and good," said the representative, wiping his glasses with a silk handkerchief. "But haven't you heard the news? Salaar's no longer our problem."

* * *

That same day, in the barracks where more than a hundred prisoners waited to be shipped to their doom, a Lycocian soldier, a tall gray fox wearing an MP armband, came in with a piece of paper.

"Here it goes," said Gilyar to Elor. "The first list of prisoners up for transport."

The soldier didn't hear Gilyar's remark. Instead, he began to read from the paper.

"On behalf of Prime Minister Jord Lak and the Parliament of the Democratic Republic of Lycocia, I am here to announce that you have all been granted asylum as of 0600 hours on this the 30th Lai, 1704. You will each be issued one one-way bus ticket to the destination of your choice. Welcome to Lycocia." He saluted sharply, then walked on to the next barracks to deliver the same news to the rest of the detainees.

The dazed creatures looked at each other in silent surprise. Some creatures grabbed their belongings and headed to the door; others sat, unsure of what had just happened.

Alrie was one such creature. She had yet to even come to terms with being denied asylum, now this? What was she to make of her life having no value one moment and having the basic dignity of asylum the next?

Elor, meanwhile, was among those creatures gathering their belongings. He took the young ferret by her hand, looking into her frightened eyes.

"It's okay, Alrie. It's all over now, we're safe," he said. Alrie couldn't say a word; she gazed at him, barely able to comprehend what the panther had just said.

"Come on now, they'll be running us out of here in a moment. Let's go find Vinz," said Elor.

At this, Alrie seemed to brighten up. She stood up and they walked out the door, hand in hand, into the bright sunlit afternoon, the first either had enjoyed as free creatures in a very long time.

Epilogue

Only when Alrie and Elor were reunited with Vinz and Laz at the hotel later that evening did they learn what had happened.

Emperor Salaar was dead, and only a week after their arrival at the Immigration Processing Center in Dunham, a violent civil war had erupted in the former Great Wolven Imperium. They were no longer simply refugees from a despotic regime, but refugees from a country that effectively no longer existed.

The civil war exposed deep divisions within the former GWI. With the emperor dead and no clear successor, there was a power vacuum to be filled and it became anyone's war.

Initially there were only two forces: the oligarchs led by Jaigon Klanar, and the military led by Air Minister Vinyon, but the situation became more complicated when other forces joined the fray.

Among them the Worker's Solidarity Front who managed to paralyze the oligarch's plans in several cities by organizing the factory workers. The New Kanil Rebels, who were a radical fringe group looking to restore the Kanil Empire, soon joined the fight.

Then there was a group whose existence surprised everyone: the Royalists, loyal to the old constitutional monarchy of King Brannagh IX.

From a studio in Greenhill, southeast Lycocia, King Brannagh began a series of regular broadcasts to the Royalists, promising the restoration of the constitution and parliament, new limitations of power for cabinet ministers, and amnesty for the political prisoners of Emperor Salaar's regime.

Fil Barron's remains, meanwhile, were given no easy rest.

Much to Elor's dismay, he learned that his skeleton had been given to the Medical University of Birchdale in West Lycocia after a fierce bidding war. The bones of a hero had been sold for a handful of banknotes.

Elor set about trying to get on as a professor of biology at said university, but after months of disappointments was only able to get work as a low-paid assistant to the dean of student affairs, hundreds of miles away in a small public university in Riverlea.

He bought a modest, comfortable house in a quiet neighborhood and moved in with Laz and Alrie; after some weeks of balking, Vinz finally joined, and in time he came to accept- however reluctantly- that Laz loved him as much as he loved Elor.

Vinz and Laz then promptly made amends with each other... from a suitably horizontal position.

It was shortly after Vinz had joined them, just as the last of the autumn leaves were about to fall, that two items arrived by post, both addressed to Elor. The first was a letter from Kerro, hand-written on what looked to be expensive stationery:

Dear Elor,

You might have guessed, the whiskey racket isn't so good these days; what with this civil war and all, nobody cares about bootlegging any more and now any old fool can make gin in their bathtub. The Nightwatch have their hands full going after all these rebel groups and no one cares about what you're drinking or smoking any more.

But it's not all bad. If I've learned anything in my life it's that there is always money to be made selling things you're not supposed to have. I've been turning a good living as a gun runner for the Cylinderheads lately. The Worker's Solidarity Front, the New Kanils, the Royalists, they all buy from me, and I give them what they need to keep up with the suits and the army. I guess you could say I'm a good guy- sort of.

I've got a nice new place just west of Northarbour, used to belong to a general. Let's just say he won't be needing it any more. The New Kanils got him with a car bomb and left a nice crater in the driveway; I still find pieces of that limousine every time I go outside.

When things settle down over here, I may have a few jobs for you. Hope you still have those names and numbers I gave you; if you ever need anything at all, one of those contacts can probably get it for you, at the same price the Cylinderheads would pay.

It was a joy working with you. I've never seen a creature in your line of work with such an amazing amount of dumb luck. Keep in touch, kid, we might be needing you again.

-Kerro

Elor pinned back his ears and growled as he read it.

"What is it?" said Vinz.

"It's nothing," he said, pulling out a small cigarette lighter and flicking it a few times. He threw the burning letter into the fireplace, letting the hated reminder of his past vanish in a cloud of gray smoke.

The other item that had arrived that day was of more interest, though. Elor turned his attention to the box. It was plain, with no return address and only minimal postage.

"Are you sure you want to open that?" asked Vinz. "With some of the characters you dealt with on the basecraft that might be the last thing you do."

Elor just shook his head. "I'll take my chances," he said, slitting the box open.

Inside was a slightly smaller box, and a folded letter:

Took me weeks to get this. Security in the biology collection is tight but I managed to get in when they weren't looking.

I had heard about what happened on the Cirrostratus and how your life was saved. I think the Medical University can do without one human skeleton, seeing as they already have half a dozen.

Anyhow, knowing what he went through, I know you'll do the right thing and give him a proper burial.

The letter was unsigned, but Elor didn't care. He held the smaller box to his chest and began to cry. "What is it, Catts?" said Vinz, placing a hand on Elor's shoulder.

Elor wiped a tear from the corner of his eye. "Get a shovel," he said softly.

Later that evening, as the sun blazed orange on the horizon, Elor, Vinz, Laz, and Alrie stood on a hill overlooking the scenic pasture lands outside of Riverlea.

In the shade of an ancient oak tree Elor put his shovel to the ground and began to dig. Alrie then handed him a small cardboard box.

With reverence, he placed the box in the earth, and for only the second time in as many decades began softly mumbling an old Inakara prayer.

> *May the Saints bless always.*
> *May the Tree of Ages from whence we are sprung shade you forever.*
> *May Ovego's shield protect you from all perils along your twilight pilgrimage.*
> *And may the Great Truth forever say of you, "He Is."*

With that, he took the first handful of dirt and dropped it reverently on the box. Alrie followed suit.

There were few other words that could be said, and the four creatures carried on in silence until Elor stood over the grave, ready to begin filling it.

"Thank you," he said. "Thank you."

www.ingramcontent.com/pod-product-compliance
Lightning Source LLC
Chambersburg PA
CBHW071250130626
46556CB00003B/1253